ABSI

SEB DOUBINSKY

ABSINTH
A NOVEL

DALKEY ARCHIVE PRESS

Library of Congress Cataloging-in-Publication Data

Names: Doubinsky, Sãebastien, 1963- author.
Title: Absinth / Seb Doubinsky.
Description: First Dalkey Archive Edition. | Victoria, TX : Dalkey Archive
 Press, 2016.
Identifiers: LCCN 2016031194 | ISBN 9781628971552 (pbk. : alk. paper)
Subjects: | GSAFD: Apocalyptic fantasies. | Fantasy fiction.
Classification: LCC PQ2664.O846 A27 2016 | DDC 843/.914--dc23
LC record available at https://lccn.loc.gov/2016031194

ILLINOIS
ARTS
COUNCIL
AGENCY

Partially funded by a grant by the Illinois Arts Council, a state agency

www.dalkeyarchive.com

Victoria, TX / McLean, IL / Dublin

Dalkey Archive Press publications are, in part, made possible through the support of the University of Houston-Victoria and its program in creative writing, publishing, and translation.

Printed on permanent/durable acid-free paper

To Michael Moorcock,
without whom the universes would not have been
the same.

Special thanks to Jean-François Mariotti
and to my wife Sofie, for their never-ending support.

spilled my own blood
in every stream I run
like a golden sword
it's all coming down
    Bardo Pond, "Destroying Angel"

And the third angel sounded, and there fell a great star
from heaven, burning as it were a lamp, and it fell upon
the third part of the rivers, and upon the fountains of
waters; And the name of the star is called Wormwood:
and the third part of the waters became wormwood; and
many men died of the waters, because they were made
bitter.
    Revelation, 8:10-11

This novel has been written using exclusively
Williams "Aqua Velva"TM.

"KEEPS YOUR FACE FIRM, TONED AND FIT."

The Heavenly Corporation

IRIS WAS IN heaven. Or almost. At the gates, at least. Opening her eyes she could see the blue sky invade her pupils, burning them terribly with its beautiful color. How many times had she seen the sky like that? The quiet laughter of the water around her accompanied her thoughts. What a trip. She took a drag of the reefer and relaxed. This was the best job she ever had. She'd had her doubts at first. Being a cleaning woman wasn't her first ambition, but hey, she had to earn a living somehow. Well, until she had become the great RnB star she wanted to become.

An ironic smile graced her face. No need to think about that right now. She just had to enjoy the peace and quiet Mrs. Denton-Smith had left her with for the whole weekend. That mean old bitch. Always complaining and threatening to fire her.

The air mattress rocked and turned on the smooth surface of the swimming pool. Iris felt a faint breeze run over her naked body. Not a bad body either. She'd had to protect it from five music agents since she had come to Petersburg. She wasn't a virgin, no sir, not even a devout Catholic, but she liked to choose whom she bedded without a price tag attached to her toe. This didn't seem common in the business, but that's the way she was.

The reefer was on its final inch and Iris inhaled the last of the medicine. "Nairobi red," Eddie had said. "Be careful," he'd added. Sure, Eddie. Whatever. She could face the heavenly music, no prob. She relaxed and swallowed the tiny bit of burnt paper and weed. Her ex-boyfriend had taught her to do that. He said the remaining weed would slowly decompose in her blood and make the buzz last longer. He was a Rasta so he should've known. The way he'd talked made her think he'd swallowed too many of those last reefer bits.

She closed her eyes and suddenly she was on another boat. The smell of pinewood was strong and mingled with the pungent scent of the ocean. For she was on the ocean now. On this old wooden ship which smelled of pinewood and manure. Yes, she thought of a zoo. Looking around she saw wooden cages harboring all kinds of animals.

Noah's ark, Iris thought. I'm on fucking Noah's ark!

She took a few steps on the deck until she heard some voices. A group of young men in robes, looking like Arabs, were pointing and talking excitedly in a strange language.

I can't believe this! It's the moment they're seeing land again!

Excited in her turn, she quietly walked up to them, forgetting she was stark naked. The thought hit her at the moment she reached the railing next to one of the guys. She instinctively put her hands over her breasts, her mouth forming a shocked "Oh!" but they didn't seem to mind. In fact, she realized with astonishment, they couldn't see her.

This is wild! I'll have to tell Eddie about this!

Reassured about her decency, she looked in the direction of the pointing fingers. It wasn't land they had noticed. It was a woman sitting on a floating piece of wood, cradling a child and looking exhausted. One of her arms was extended toward the ship, and she was shouting words the wind seemed to carry away. Iris noticed she was dressed in a deep blue garment made of torn and dirty fabric. Her face was dark, Ethiopian-looking, a little bit like her own, as a matter of fact. The baby was bundled up like a tiny mummy and only a small black hand gripping the mother's robe indicated its presence.

Iris felt her heart beat faster. She was going to witness a rescue. It was more exciting than coming to land. She couldn't help waving to the woman and her baby, shouting words of encouragement, although she was pretty sure they couldn't hear her.

Silence fell and Iris turned around. An old man had joined the group. He was disheveled, his face hidden by a mountain of white hair and a huge beard of the same hue. He wore a dirty robe and his eyes seemed to be burning with insane fire.

Iris felt her knees grow weak. Noah himself! Fucking A!

This was the wildest trip she'd experienced since her first acid trip, when she had turned sixteen. But then she had only talked to John Lennon.

Noah listened to the others' excited explanations and took a quick look. The woman had floated away. The distance made her seem smaller and Iris couldn't hear her cries any more. They had to act fast, Iris thought, just like in a movie. Suspense in real life. The best.

But Noah just shrugged, said a few angry words, spat on the ground and left. The young men looked at each other, silent. Slowly, the group broke apart and Iris found herself alone on this part of the deck. The woman was nothing but a fat black dot now, bobbing up and down on the horizon, getting smaller minute by minute.

It was the motion that pulled her gaze away from the desperate shape. She opened her eyes and the sky attacked them with a vengeance. The pungent smell of animals had been replaced by the sharp, acidic scent of chlorine. She was back floating on the swimming pool.

What a trip! she thought. I have to tell the others.

Then she remembered Eddie and anger filled her soul. That motherfucker had given her a joint laced with something. He would hear about that. She could have done some crazy things, like jump from the roof of her building or think she could breathe underwater. What kind of manager would do that, anyway, try to kill his future star?

But still, what a trip!

The Lone Highway

THE SKY WAS metal blue and the yellow hills shimmered in the heat. The duffel bag on his shoulder weighed a ton. There were no vultures circling over him, but they wouldn't be long. Marco had never imagined 50,000 dollars in small bills could be this heavy. He stopped and turned around. He couldn't see the car anymore. Only the plume of black smoke, a few miles back, that went straight up. How could one crash on a straight line? He tried a painful smile. Blood clogged his eyelids and he wasn't too sure whether his right arm was broken. It dangled numb and useless by his side, yet he could feel his fingers, although he couldn't move them. What had Sid's wife said? Oh, yeah: An easy job.

And it had been easy, all right. Saperstein was a sucker. Always has been, always will be. He shouldn't have refused Marco his raise, though. All he was asking for was a hundred bucks. Times were getting tough. Everybody was struggling. And Marco wasn't getting any younger either. The big four-oh in a couple of months. Couldn't easily just quit and go get exploited somewhere else. Age wasn't equaled by experience anymore.

When Sid's wife had appeared at his doorstep two weeks ago it was like a fucking miracle. Offered him exactly what he needed. Money and revenge.

He had worked for Saperstein eleven years. Not exactly the junior and yet Saperstein hadn't even let him finish. "No," he'd said "I don't give myself a raise, so why would I give you one?" Smartass. Who was sorry now?

Marco secured the heavy bag on his shoulder and dragged himself slowly on. A car would be coming soon. Or a pickup truck. Or a truck. Or something. The cops, maybe. He almost laughed at that one. His hair was on fire. Salty sweat ran into his eyes. His body hurt in a thousand places. He didn't care. If he died now, he would die a rich man. And that, in itself, was an achievement.

Publish and Perish

SID SAPERSTEIN FELT a cold sweat wrap his back as if someone had given him a very damp towel after a very hot shower.

"Whaddya mean, we're missing page 261? But that's the last page, isn't it?"

He thought he was going to scream but his voice came out an asthmatic wheeze.

"On all 350,000 of them?"

The voice on the other end of the line confirmed.

"Fuck! Fuck! FUCK!"

He banged the phone down, startling Miss Jenkins. She had been kneeling under the desk the whole time, her mouth half open, feeling Sid grow limp in her hand.

"That's 75,000 dollars down the drain! Fuck! Where's Marco, that son of a bitch? What do I pay him for?"

"He didn't show up today," Miss Jenkins's voice said from below. "He didn't even call in sick."

Sid pondered this, drumming his fingers on the desk, fuming. He still owed Tonio a hundred grand and he'd hoped that Bloodstained Virgins would make back a good deal of the money, considering its author had died in a freak accident and had no family. A hundred percent profit.

He should've known better than to play Texas Hold 'em with his father-in-law. Hell, Tonio was good, but he hadn't known he was that good. They'd often played in the past, and he'd either come out even or a little under. Nothing lethal. But now . . . He wondered if Maria's filing for divorce had anything to do with that. Maria . . .

On their wedding day, Tonio had wanted to speak to him face to face.

"I don't know what you see in my daughter, because even I, her father, can't see it. But if you need any money, just ask."

Well, he had actually liked Maria, even though she was a little bit on the plump side, not very intelligent, and prone to hysterics. But she had been the first woman who hadn't been shocked by the books he was publishing. Vinland Press had two major fields: porn and pulp. "The two Ps," as Sid would proudly say, "that clash with Pride and Prejudice, those bourgeois notions." Actually, Maria had liked the books so much, he'd eventually asked her to become a volunteer editor, shoving manuscripts on their night table that she would skim through eating chips on even dates and candy on odd ones.

Her remarks and choices had always been good, and he had quickly made a fortune. When the illustrated books came out—another of her ideas—Vinland Press had suddenly become the most fashionable seedy publishing house in Petersburg. Until five years ago, when a series of flops, added to harsh competition, had sent them waltzing by the side of the publishing world again. Sid tried to make a comeback, but bad luck seemed to follow him like a shark follows a trail of blood. He blamed it all on Maria—most of the flops were her choices, anyway, as he seldom read more than the first five pages of any manuscript—and their marriage began to look increasingly like an English bomber flying on one engine over Berlin during World War Two.

It was more than regrettable that, about ten days ago, after a sour break-up, a disgruntled mistress had sent Maria some revealing pictures of herself and Sid having fun at a motel. He remembered taking pictures on her digital camera, but he didn't think they would someday find their way to a color laser printer . . .

Maria hadn't made a scene. Instead, he'd found their house empty but for her lawyer sitting in the big leather armchair in front of the fake fireplace. The lawyer handed Sid a large brown envelope containing copies of the pictures, the letter accompanying them, and a whole bunch of legal papers concerning a divorce.

The following day Tonio had invited him to the infamous poker game. "To change your mind," the soon to be ex-father-in-law had said. Well, it didn't really work out that way. When Sid finally decided to quit, around five o'clock in the morning, Tonio told him he shouldn't worry too much about the money, that he had a whole two weeks to come up with it. That was a week ago. He suddenly wondered if Maria had something to do with the missing pages. Could she and Marco be involved?

Suddenly, feeling dizzy from so many bad thoughts, Sid slapped the wooden surface with the flat of his hands, making the pencils do half a turn in their cup.

"Let's go eat something. A good steak is what I need right now!"

He packed the meat back in, pulled the zipper, and got up. Miss Jenkins stood up in her turn, careful not to bump her head. There was no point adding ridicule to disaster.

Old Friends

"AND YOU'RE SURE this is information we can trust?" Legba asked, pouring a double dose of rum into the shot glasses.

The Haitian God of Crossroads and Changes was dressed in an impeccable white Dolce & Gabbana suit, his silver-pommeled cane hanging on his left arm.

Hermes, the Greek god of the same trade, dressed in a pigeon-gray Sonia Rykiel suit with matching hat, shrugged and lifted the glass to his lips. They were sitting on Legba's terrace, overlooking Port-au-Prince's chaotic silhouette.

"I don't know. But it would make sense. I'm sure you've felt things too."

Legba reclined in his chair and sighed.

"Funny how we can predict the future for single mortals, but we can't see our own."

"The Rules of the Universe, or what's left of them," replied Hermes. "Maybe we should ask mortals to predict our future. That's never been done before."

"Well, Karl Marx and Friedrich Nietzsche sort of did, didn't they?" Legba said, taking out a hand-rolled cigar from a beautifully-crafted box.

He offered it to Hermes, who shook his head.

"No, I only smoke cigarettes. Yes, and they were both wrong."

"Don't know if that's entirely true. But I see what you mean. Still, what you told me is . . . unexpected. At the very least. Who's your informant?"

"Pythia, who else?"

Legba closed his eyes for a second, and a faint smile crossed his lips.

"Yes, who else? That damned woman! She's still good, isn't she?"

"Good as new. And still butt ugly and insane too."

The gods laughed quietly in unison. The mixed smells of the city drifted up to the balcony. Hermes turned his strange, slightly off-center, pale green gaze toward the mad urban maze twisting at the foot of the hill. Mortals. Can't live with them, can't survive without them.

He heard the click of the lighter, then the burst of the flame. A sour smoke tickled his nostrils. In the past, it would have been a pleasure. But now smells, like all the other sensations, were more like faded memories. Regrets, to be precise. Legba's face disappeared behind a cloud of blue smoke.

He remembered when Pythia had called him from Athens and asked him to pay her a visit. He also remembered the disgusting apartment near Plaka, full of loose birds and crazy-eyed cats. She'd made him the worst coffee he had ever tasted and, as he'd told Legba, she really was an ugly mother. But she'd told him about the signs. The slight change in the wind's direction. The tides rolling in a little faster. What the birds were singing. What the electricity was whispering. It all made sense.

Something was happening, at last. They had been waiting for it for thousands of years. Someone was creeping onto Jove's territory. And the Rules of the Universe could maybe fall back to what they used to be. Hermes felt goosebumps run up his arms.

The idea of making love with mortals again.

The possibility of favoring or punishing whom you bloody wanted to.

To discuss endlessly with a fellow traveler at a crossroads.

To bring gifts or send a disease.

To choose a side during a war.

The thought of all these possibilities coming back — soon — made him want to cry.

"What are you thinking about?" Legba asked, his voice thickened by the cigar smoke.

"The Rules of the Universe, what else?"

Legba smiled.

"Yes, indeed, what else?"

Legba looked at his friend reclining on the balcony's railing. The Rules of the Universe. What god, what loa, what spirit wasn't thinking about them now? Before Jove had appeared and made a name for himself, everybody talked about them and nobody knew what they were about. Only the effects. Not the causes. And men and gods had lived happily side by side. Most of the time, at least. Of course, it had always been a little bit better for the gods.

But Jove showed up out of nowhere and played a smart game. He told men a couple of lies about the other gods, scared them shitless, and it worked. Quick game too. A couple of thousand years and he had almost won the entire market, sending the Old Guys back to their farms, deserts, hills, jungles, and ponds — for those who had been lucky. But the Old Bastards weren't finished yet. Things had come up. New things, from the old. And the Rules of the Universe would fall back to what they once were. And should have always remained.

A Minor Incident

THE CYCLIST, A young man in his early thirties, was carelessly riding on the sidewalk, his MP3 player blasting into his ears, returning from the interior design firm where he worked as a junior.

He was casually dressed for the summer, wearing a pair of baggy shorts and a white sleeveless t-shirt, a strap bag across his stomach filled with bio products. To him, riding a bike in a city filled with cars was an act of rebellion and he was proud of it. He believed in fighting capitalism in all its forms and was against the death penalty. He thought women were equal to men, although he regretted that they weren't easier to bed. He believed fast food chains were trying to poison the entire planet and that saving tap water was good. Still, he didn't see the five-year-old walking out of the grocer's, proudly carrying the ice cream his mother had just bought him.

It was an unusually hot summer day, a direct consequence of global warming. Until now, the cyclist had gracefully avoided all the annoying pedestrians who strolled on the sidewalk. Of course, he should have ridden by the curb, but then again, traffic was too dangerous.

That stupid kid should have looked when he walked out. His mother should have warned him. What kind of education are the kids getting nowadays? He came out running. The cyclist didn't even have time to brake. He hit the kid sideways, so hard he fell from the bike, doing a somersault over the handlebars. Hurt himself badly too.

The kid was thrown against the wall, head slamming into the concrete. Blood ran from his crown, and oozed from his lips. The mother screamed. Passersby froze. The cyclist tried to stand up, but was disoriented from the shock. His hands and knees hurt. Stupid kid. The boy didn't move, eyes showing white. His t-shirt was stained with a mixture of blood and strawberry ice cream. His mother kneeled beside him and cradled him like a Mater Dolorosa, her face blank with shock.

The cyclist finally managed to get up and said he was sorry. The mother didn't answer. She was talking to her kid, trying to make him wake up. The young man said sorry again, louder this time, but there was no reaction.

A crowd had gathered. The cyclist saw that the kid was alive, although his face was caked with blood. His breathing was faint, but a pink bubble appeared every now and then at the corner of his mouth.

Hearing the distant sound of a siren in the background, the cyclist felt relieved. Help was on its way.

A man was kneeling beside the mother and taking a look at the kid. He said he was the local pharmacist. Perfect. Although his own body hurt like hell, his knees and hands all bloody from the fall, the cyclist decided that everything was more or less under control now. He hoped this would teach the kid a good lesson—and the mother too.

The cyclist tried to mount his bike again, but a man prevented him from doing so. Surprised, he attempted to mount again, with the same result. Only there were two men now, holding him back. Who the fuck did these dudes think they were? The cyclist tried to push one of the guys away, but the guy pushed him back and the cyclist fell flat on his backside.

Now he was angry. He shuffled to his feet, but a kick in the stomach threw him back on the ground again. The siren was getting closer. There was another one now. He hoped one of the vehicles would be the cops. He would press charges. He would send the bastards to jail. Trying to ignore the flashes of pain, he got back on all fours. A hand suddenly pulled him by the hair and dragged him into the middle of the street.

"Hey!" The cyclist screamed. "Hey!"

In shock, he turned his head just in time to see his bike being thrown at him by an old man. He ducked, but the heavy frame hit him sideways in the forehead, stunning him. The crowd was thicker now and he could hear screams and insults directed at him.

"What's going on?" he whined, his mouth now filled with the metallic taste of blood. "I didn't hit the kid on purpose. He should've looked where he was going . . ."

A kick in the face snapped his mouth shut, shattering his teeth. A hurricane of blows, kicks, and spit fell down on him. The bike was thrown on his unconscious body several more times, until one of the wheels was completely twisted.

Finally, in the good old lynching tradition, somebody dragged the semiconscious body by the hair to the foot of a streetlamp. Others lifted him up and he was hanged, along with the bike, and then both were set on fire.

When the police and ambulance finally arrived at the scene, only a small group of onlookers stood around the mother and her injured child. When questioned, they all said there was nothing they could do to prevent the lynching and no, they wouldn't be able to identify anyone. The mother was softly singing a lullaby. The song only stopped when the doors of the ambulance closed. The police had to call the fire department to extinguish the burning body and bicycle. It was a good forty-five minutes before everything returned to normal.

GOD SAYS:

THESE STYLE TRAILBLAZERS ARE SETTING
THEIR SIGHTS ON SOCIAL CAUSES WITH
PROVOCATIVE DOCUMENTARIES

The Heavenly Corporation

BACK AT HER one-room apartment, Iris was fuming and on the verge of tears. The audition had been terrible. Okay, it was for a stupid TV show. Show Me Yours and I'll Show You Mine. How could you call a show that? Anyway, it was supposed to make you instantly famous. You had to sing naked and they would give you a record contract if you won the competition. Of course the auditions were filmed. And of course there were thousands of candidates. But Eddie had thought it would be a good idea. Maybe she wouldn't win, but perhaps some club owner would notice her and contact her anyway.

Yeah, as if.

Well, she undressed and she sang. She sang very well, in fact, but they laughed. The jury laughed at her. They mocked her "natural" look. They hinted that she had come directly from the jungle. At first, confused, she thought they were being openly racist. It was only when one of the so-called judges asked what it was like to wear a toupee in the wrong place that she understood.

She hadn't trimmed her bush or shaved her armpits. Her legs, yes, she always did. But the rest, no. She hadn't even thought about that.

And now, she knew she would be on TV tonight, and that would be the ruin of her career. Fuck, she hoped nobody would watch that bloody program. Nobody important, at least.

She got up from her couch, a crumpled tissue in her hand, and walked to the small dining table. She took a half-smoked joint from the ashtray and lit it.

At least she knew dope would never let her down.

The Lone Highway

MARCO WAS SITTING by the side of the road, exhausted. The large bag lay next to him, useless. What he needed now wasn't 50,000 dollars. What he needed now was water and a miracle. It was like a fucking parable. If he hadn't been in so much pain, he would have laughed out loud.

There was an old movie with a similar story, he remembered. By a German dude. It was called The Vultures or something like that. Three bad guys chasing some treasure in the desert, all dying in the end. Black and white. Silent? He couldn't remember.

Suddenly, in the distance, he saw some smoke. Another accident? This sure was a dangerous road. He painfully got to his feet again. No, it wasn't smoke. It was dust. A cloud of dust coming his way. He felt his heart beat faster. The Indians or the 7th Cavalry?

A car was approaching. Fast. So fast he hesitated a moment to wave, thinking it would never stop. It was black, a '70s Cadillac Seville, just like in gangster movies.

Perfect, Marco thought. Now, I'm going to get a ride with the Mob . . .

He signaled anyway, the bag still at his feet. The car didn't slow down, just kept coming on in its cloud of dust.

Maybe he's being chased by the cops. That would be grand.

Marco kept flagging the car with his uninjured arm, hoping he didn't look too weird from the other side of the windscreen. But the car flew past him, sending dust and gravel particles into his eyes and open mouth.

"Son of a bitch!" Marco cried out loud. "Motherfucking son of a bitch!"

As if the driver had heard him, the car came to a screeching halt about a hundred feet away. Marco wiped his eyes and spit out bad-tasting dust. The car seemed to be waiting for him.

Grumbling insults, Marco picked up his bag and, wincing from the pain, ran as fast as he could to the car. When he reached the passenger's side, he waited for the door to open, but instead the smoked-glass window rolled down.

Peering inside, Marco saw the driver's face thrust toward him. The guy didn't look Italian. Actually, he looked like a Nazi bastard, so blond he could be albino, but his eyes weren't red — they were ice blue and seemed to glow in the car's gloomy interior. He wore a large silver crucifix hanging outside his half-open shirt.

"Is that your car up the road?" the man asked, with a weird, unidentifiable accent.

Norwegian, Marco thought.

"Yes, it is. I was very lucky," he added. "I could have been killed."

"Indeed you were," the stranger agreed.

Marco waited for the door to open, but instead the stranger opened his glove compartment, looking for something.

"I'm glad you stopped. I haven't seen a bloody car in the last five hours. God must have sent you."

Leaning back on his seat, the stranger gave a wry smile.

"Exactly," he said, leveling his automatic and shooting Marco straight in the face.

The Heavenly Corporation

AARON LOOKED AT his watch. The sun was hiding behind the huge mass of Mount Sinai, turning everything blue. He was worried for his brother. The storm at the top of the mountain had lasted a week now and he was afraid Moses would never come back down. He'd set up an effigy of Apis, the Golden Bull, to protect his brother, and they'd sacrificed twenty black sheep to ask for the favor of the god. Of course Moses wouldn't approve. Since he had found this new god, Jove or whatever his name was, he'd become exceedingly impatient with all other forms of worship, from the legitimate Egyptian deities to the more obscure Phoenician and Nubian ones. Everything had to make way for a god who didn't even have a name — Jove was just a pseudonym, supposedly. Still, Aaron liked the old gods and knew he could count on them. After all, they had protected them during their exile in Egypt, hadn't they? Where was that silent god then?

The sound system installed behind the wooden effigy of Apis, the heavenly bull, resounded in the distance. The mixed smells of incense and weed tickled Aaron's nose and he looked down at the valley where the festivities were going on.

Once again Moses had left him behind to talk to that faceless, nameless being who cockily called himself "God." Sure, he'd made some miracles — but then again, which god hadn't? Every morning Osiris brought back the sun—and that was enough, wasn't it? He heard chanting from below. The twelve tribes were having a great time, reassured by rites they knew well. And they liked Moses, although he was a strange old man. They wanted him protected and the rite they were performing was the strongest of all protection rites. Hopefully Moses would see though his madness and come to his senses.

Aaron was happy they had come out of Egypt — politics had turned recently and the wave of anti-Semitism that had struck the country sure was bad news. But it had happened before.

He couldn't help feeling sorry for the disasters Moses's god had plagued his motherland with . . . The toads, the bloody river, the locusts. And the babies. Especially the babies. Aaron loved children. When he heard the wailing in the streets and saw the mothers dressed in white and the hundreds of funerals going on at the same time in the various temples and cemeteries, his eyes had filled with tears. Moses had locked himself up in his room the whole time. Aaron knocked on the door, but all he could hear was Moses's voice mumbling and chanting. He thought his brother had finally gone mad for good. Even hoped he had, maybe. What kind of god massacred children? Surely only men did that, but then again, men were mad. It was embedded in their nature, in their soul. But a god?

Aaron had doubted since then, although he hadn't told his brother. Moses scared him. Scared him bad. Aaron had to talk for him, because of his harelip and his lisp, and he made sure he repeated exactly what Moses told him to, because he didn't want to be struck by lightning or, worse, eaten alive by cockroaches, or whatever other atrocious death Moses's god could come up with.

Two patrolling guards from the Levite tribe strolled quietly by, their shotguns cradled in their arms. They waved at Aaron, who waved back. Moses had said the Levites would be in charge of security. Why them? Because Jove said so. And he couldn't have chosen better: the Levites were all violent half-wits, who were more than delighted when Aaron pulled up in front of their tents with the van full of guns. Where had Moses found the weapons? Yet another mystery. But here the Levites were, with their crazy beards, patrolling the perimeter in their fatigues.

Aaron hoped Moses would come back soon. Things were getting a little out of control back at the camp. People had obviously enjoyed getting back to Apis and the ancient rituals. The air was thick with the smoke of dope and the smell of lust. It also shimmered with joy and relief. Aaron couldn't ignore that, and it made him feel slightly better. After all, it was he who had decided to go back to the ancient ways. Moses did need protection.

Aaron pensively watched the backs of the Levites slowly strolling downhill, their guns reflecting no light in the dying sun. Suddenly he wasn't so sure he would be happy to see Moses again.

As if on cue, he spotted the heavy silhouette of his brother emerging from the thick fog which had settled on the mountain when Moses left to talk to his god at the top. Moses carried what looked like a heavy flat stone in each arm — Aaron first thought of small tombstones.

He rushed to help his brother, glad to see he was alive and unhurt, although his hair and beard were a mess and some of his clothing was torn apart. Aaron was a few feet away from his brother when he saw Moses freeze. The look on Moses's face made him stop in his tracks.

"What the fuck?" Moses yelled, running down the slope, his steps made uncertain because of the weight of the stones. "What the fuck is going on?"

"These are the words of God, Aaron!" the old man shouted, only the weight of the tablets in his arms preventing an eruption of fury. "And you betrayed me! You betrayed everybody! You betrayed God!"

With an inhuman scream, Moses threw the tablets on the ground, where they broke into pieces, then he ran toward the camp. Aaron tried to stop him, but Moses took a step back and punched him square in the face. Aaron felt a blinding pain as his nose cracked under the blow and he doubled over at the feet of his older brother. Moses savagely kicked him in the ribs and stomach a couple of times, leaving him lying on the ground gasping for air, as a pool of vomit spread under his cheek.

"Moses, wait! Wait!" he managed to shout, as the furious man tramped away.

Aaron slowly lifted his arm, as if to stop Moses by magic, but the old gods were powerless. He heard his brother's growl of despair turn into a rage-filled scream. The Levite brothers rallied behind him, running like a pack of faithful wolves.

Aaron felt his heart sink as he watched the little troop disappear down the hill. From the camp, he could still hear the music booming and the chants and laughter of the party going on.

"You don't understand," Aaron whispered. "You don't understand. It was to protect you."

Aaron tried to pick himself up, but the pain was too intense and he fell heavily back onto his side, his mouth sticky with a mixture of blood, vomit, and dirt. He heard the music stop and a tremendous silence fall upon the evening. He heard Moses's voice gain strength like a hurricane, unintelligible fragments of his tirade reaching his ears through the filter of the wind. Then the firecracker sounds of the guns. Again and again. People screamed. Aaron felt sick to his stomach. Moses was punishing them for something he had suggested. Was there no justice? He heard the great statue of Apis toppled in a great crash.

It was all over.

They had a new god now.

Through his pain, Aaron wondered what Jove had written on Moses's stone tablets.

Crawling slowly, he managed to reach the broken stones. Wincing, he extended his fingers and turned a chunk over with great pain and difficulty.

It was completely blank.

Just before fainting, he thought he saw the silhouette of a black woman looking at him. He feebly extended a hand toward her, but she shimmered and disappeared like a ghost.

An Olympic Tragedy
Part One

"THANK YOU FOR joining us live for the fiftieth summer Olympics men's diving competition. The sun is shining high over Athens, and inside the aquatic complex conditions are perfect, aren't they, Steve?"

"Well, yes, Frank, they sure are."

"For those who have just joined us, the Chinese twenty-year-old, Han Men, is leading the competition, closely followed by the twenty-one-year-old Ukrainian, Davidenko, and the eighteen-year-old American, Harris. It is now the turn of the other Chinese competitor, Hou Tsi, he's had a very good season this year, hasn't he, Steve?"

"Yes, very good indeed."

"In fact, he's the favorite for this competition. Do you think he can seriously challenge Han Men, Davidenko, and Harris, Steve?"

"Undoubtedly."

"Well, here he is, getting ready. Spectacular body and quite tall for a Chinese, isn't he. Six feet is quite uncommon among Asians, I hear."

"Well, there are some Cambodians who are pretty tall, as well as some Japanese, mostly from the northern islands. There are also records of tall Koreans and Indonesians. And . . ."

"Thank you, Steve. Hou Tsi is concentrating. What do you think he's thinking about right now? A gold medal?"

"What else? The democratization of his country?"

"Ha, ha, very funny, Steve! I knew you would say something like that! There he goes now! What the?"

" . . ."

"That wasn't a dive! He, he just jumped straight down in the water . . ."

" . . ."

"What do you think happened, Steve? And wait . . . He's not coming up . . . He appears to be sitting at the bottom of the pool . . . What the hell is he doing? Trying to break the free-diving world record?"

"Ha! Ha! Ha! That's a good one!"

"No, seriously . . . It's getting dangerous . . . They're sending in two divers now . . . This is just incredible . . . They're trying to move him I can see, but he's resisting . . . They're trying to make him surface . . . It looks like Hou Tsi is screaming something in the water . . . Can we get the underwater camera? Can you read lips, Steve?"

"No, I'm afraid I can't. What's more, it's probably in Chinese . . ."

"Of course. He seems unconscious now, whatever his message was. They're pulling him out of the water . . . The medics are here. They're rolling him onto his side . . . Still not moving . . . He's being examined by the medics . . . The trainer is here now, with another Chinese . . . Maybe the translator . . . They're trying a heart massage . . . The crowd is completely still . . . And believe me, a crowd of 50,000 people, completely silent, that's eerie, isn't it, Steve?"

"You took the words right out of my mouth."

"The stretcher is here, with a thermal blanket . . . I saw one of the medics shake his head . . . What do you think it means, Steve?"

"Nothing good, I'm afraid. I wonder what he was screaming. I hope the network can get an interpreter and give us more info."

"It would have to be a lip-reader who understands Chinese, and I gather they're pretty hard to find, although the Chinese are so numerous nowadays."

"Well over a billion of them. And still growing."

"Absolutely, Steve. Well, that was something. Hou Tsi has been taken to hospital, and we'll keep you posted if we have any further information while we're on air . . ."

"Especially about his message."

"Yes, right. Especially about his message. But, like we say back home, the show must go on and our next candidate is this year's European revelation, the British Wonder, Tim Angus. Do you think he can threaten any of the top three?"

GOD SAYS:

NEW
SUGAR SUGAR
LIP TOPPING
GIVE 'EM SOME SUGAR

Publish and Perish

SID WAS CHEWING on his beef sandwich, his eyes looking right through Miss Jenkins, right through the wall behind her, traveling the whole distance out of Petersburg, over the ocean, across an entire continent, then another ocean, to end up right behind his own forehead.

Miss Jenkins was struggling with her half-finished Caesar salad and wondering what her boss was thinking about. She had lost her appetite after she'd heard the bad news and couldn't understand how Sid could still eat like that when he was in so much trouble. She was wondering if he was thinking of finding money to finance a second edition of the Bloody Virgins—Sid was marvelous at that sort of thing—or if he was considering firing her to save on overheads.

Actually, Sid wasn't thinking about her at all. He was thinking about death. His own. Tonio would learn within hours of his misadventure and understand that, barring a miracle, he would never see his money again.

As if on cue, Sid felt his mobile vibrate in the inside pocket of his jacket. He continued eating his sandwich until the little melody chimed, indicating his caller had left a message.

Noticing that Miss Jenkins had finished her salad, he ordered two coffees.

He reluctantly looked at his cell phone. It was a message from Tonio: "A hundred thousand tonight, amigo."

Why did people think that the worst thing about death was that it was unpredictable? He really believed now that the contrary was much worse.

The coffees were brought and Miss Jenkins started sipping hers while Sid just sat staring at the whirling knots of steam.

"Are you OK, Mr. Saperstein?"

Miss Jenkins's voice draws up a weary gaze.

"No, not really. I'm thinking about that book. It's going to pull us down—in a big way."

"A miracle can always happen," Miss Jenkins said in a hopeful tone.

"Yes, and that's what we need right now."

The waiter came with the bill. Sid made for his wallet, but Miss Jenkins stopped him and paid for them both. This is a miracle, Sid thought. A small but real miracle. Maybe she also had a hidden fortune, he mused. Now, that sure would be the kind of miracle he needed.

Breaking News
Part One

AP, 15:01 — NEW information concerning the mysterious deaths of the president and vice president of the United States has been released. It is now believed that they both died of Ebola fever. It is still unclear how the president and vice president might have come into contact with the Ebola virus, as they have not officially traveled outside the USA in the last eight months. It has been suggested that a biological terrorist attack may have taken place on American soil, but so far government security agencies say they have no evidence to support this theory. At a press conference this morning a White House spokesman said: "Although this is an exceptional tragedy, every American can be assured that there is no known risk to the public and that the day-to-day running of our great nation is in safe hands and will continue as normal. If we establish that the deaths of our president and vice president are the result of an attack on American liberties and freedoms, that attack will be followed by swift and merciless retribution."

Breaking News
Part Two

AP, 19:34 — THE body of the Russian president was found this afternoon about five miles from where his helicopter crashed in northern Siberia. The president's remains were discovered by a group of hunters who allegedly told reporters that the frozen body looked as if it had been half-eaten by wolves. The Russian state news agency, Novosti, later issued a "correction" saying that there was no evidence the president's body had been attacked by animals. Allegations are circulating in official circles in Moscow that the helicopter was either sabotaged or shot down by Chechen rebels. So far, state security organizations, such as the FSB, have refused to comment on these rumors. Fearing that the president's death could "push Russia into chaos," the parliamentary leader said at a press conference: "The country is in good hands and the Russian people need not worry about their future."

Breaking News
Part Three

AP, 23:57 — THE deaths of the entire Central Committee of the Communist Party of China have been reported. Sources say that the cause of these deaths, when confirmed, is likely to be food poisoning. The deaths are believed to have occurred on Monday evening. Rumors of a serious incident first began to circulate on Tuesday when the annual meeting of the Committee was postponed. Committee sessions scheduled to be broadcast on the state-controlled television network were replaced by classical opera programming. The cause of the food poisoning is not yet known, but rumors are circulating in official circles of a possible act of terrorism. Muslim rebels from the south and a radical branch of the Tibetan resistance movement are seen as the most likely perpetrators. Hundreds of arrests have been reported. Chinese authorities have so far made no official comment. The secretary general of the Presidium

of the National People's Congress is scheduled to address
the nation at eight o'clock tonight and a week of official
national mourning has been proclaimed.

GOD SAYS:

THE EDGY STUDDED LOOK REVEALS ITS SOFTER SIDE THIS SEASON, AS DESIGNERS COVER SIMPLE, MONOCHROMATIC PIECES WITH DELICATE PASTEL-HUED EMBELLISHMENTS.

The Heavenly Corporation

EDDIE WAS LISTENING to her with a half smile she didn't really like. They were at his place, a small but comfortable two-room apartment overlooking Harriman Square and its never-ending traffic.

"Visions, huh?"

Iris nodded vehemently.

"Yes, visions."

"Like you can see the future?"

"No, I told you. Like I can see the past."

Eddie shrugged and lit a joint.

"Anybody can do that. They're called memories, you know."

"Not when they're scenes from the Bible. So far, I've seen Noah and the flood and Moses."

"You told me you were stoned every time. And that they weren't the stories we were told. And you said Aaron had a watch and people had guns . . . Come on!"

He handed the joint to Iris, who took a long drag.

"Yes, but the visions were real, Eddie. I was there."

"Okay, tell you what. You're going to hold my hands. If you see something I am the only one to know, then I can accept you're having visions. What do you say?"

"Deal."

Eddie extended his hands and she took a deep breath. She had never tried this before.

"Can I have another hit? It would make me more relaxed," she said, rubbing her hands on her thighs.

"Sure, whatever you want."

She took a long drag and felt her mind clear. This was exactly like in one of those movies she loved. All that clairvoyance shit.

She grabbed Eddie's fingers and closed her eyes.

It hit her like a sixteen-ton truck at full speed.

Eddie was at a gas station, filling up his old Camaro.

He finished, went to the booth and paid.

Then he left, forgetting the fuel tank cap on the roof of the car.

"So?" Eddie asked, amused.

She told him what she had seen. He lifted an eyebrow incredulously, got up, and left the apartment. Ten minutes later he was back, smelling slightly of gasoline.

"You were right," he said. "I'd forgotten it was on top of the car. Lucky for me the gas station is less than a mile from here . . ."

Iris smiled, waiting for more compliments.

"Still," he said, sitting back at the table, "it's only the past. Can't do shit with that kind of thing. What about the future?"

Iris shrugged.

"I don't know."

"Come on. Let's do it."

They pumped a little more on a new joint, giggling excitedly.

"Maybe you'll see me as your happy manager and you, you'll be a star . . ."

Iris smiled. Yes, that would be great, she thought. Especially after that fucking TV show.

She grabbed Eddie's hands and concentrated. Eyes closed, she tried to pick up vibes, waves, images, whatever, but to no avail. The only thing she saw was pitch-black darkness and she told Eddie so.

"You suck," he snapped, reclining on his couch.

That was when she decided to get rid of her manager.

Publish and Perish

BACK AT HIS office, Sid knew what to do. He told Miss Jenkins he didn't want to be disturbed and locked the door. Sweat stained the back of his shirt, and his hands were trembling slightly. He didn't like to do what he was about to do, but he didn't want to die just yet either. Maria wanted him dead and if Maria wanted him dead, then Papa Tonio would make him dead. Was it going to be an accident? A drive-by shooting? A knife in the back in the men's bathroom? Whatever, he had to leave town fast.

Sid carefully lifted the framed Betty Page poster facing the office door and looked at the built-in safe nobody else knew about. He had managed to stash about 50,000 dollars, money he'd carefully skimmed over the years despite Maria's watchful accounting. It was money he used at motels and in restaurants with his various mistresses and that one day would buy him the yacht he'd always dreamed of. Well, fuck the yacht now. It would buy him a fake passport and a one-way ticket to Babylon, Viborg City, or Constantinople, help him start a new business under a new name.

He turned the button clockwise and counterclockwise until he heard the reassuring click! Taking a deep breath, he peeked into the dark opening. He peeked again, trying to grasp what he was seeing. All the money was gone, and there was just a folded paper note. He seized the note with trembling fingers and opened it, knowing already what he would find. Ciao, sucker! was written in Maria's beautiful handwriting. Yeah, suck on this one, someone had added, with an obscene drawing. Marco, no doubt.

He was about to burst into tears when a sharp rap on the door made his heart skip a beat.

"What is it?" he yelled. "I told you I don't want to be disturbed!"

"Yes, but this man says it's of the utmost importance."

Miss Jenkins was breathless.

"Did Tonio send him?" Sid asked again, feeling the sweat bathe his forehead.

He could hear Miss Jenkins's muffled voice questioning the visitor.

"No, he says Jesus sent him."

"Jesus?"

Sid was baffled. The last thing he needed now was some religious freak.

"Tell him to come back tomorrow. I'm busy right now."

Again, he heard Miss Jenkins talking to the stranger.

"He says he can't wait and he knows you need a miracle."

The words hit Sid like a stray bullet. He closed the safe, put the framed poster back in place, and walked around his desk to open the door.

"A miracle is always welcome here," he said, letting the stranger enter his office.

Remember to Turn Off the Light
When You Leave

AT THE BEGINNING, people thought it was just a new trend, a political statement made by a few thousand disgruntled individuals to embark the West on a new guilt trip. Some thought it was a new "Back to Africa" or "Return to Roots" phenomenon, which would be short-lived and quickly forgotten.

The lack of political slogans or vengeful claims began to intrigue the Western media and politicians. Immigrants left America and Europe in scores, disrupting airports, railway stations, and harbors with their ever-increasing numbers. They waited patiently, passports at the ready, everyone from young illegal aliens to entire families who'd been in the countries for years. They waited for planes, trains, ships, buses, sometimes even cars to take them home.

They stayed silent and refused to explain their motivations to the media. Specialists appeared on TV every night to explain the situation, but none were convincing. Politicians offered solutions, non-governmental organizations suggested new laws, extremists from the right and the left rejoiced — for diametrically opposed reasons.

Of course, the home nations weren't too happy with the situation. They tried to close their borders and send the newcomers back to where they'd come from, to pass similar laws to those of the wealthy West — but to no avail. The people kept returning, settling down in towns, cities, favelas, barrios, villages, using the money they had with them to start businesses, factories, restaurants, creating much-needed wealth around them.

A few months later all those intending to go had gone, and as Western economies plummeted like never before, the wealthy nations really began to worry.

But it was more than a little too late.

The Heavenly Corporation

IRIS BOUGHT A new bookshelf for all the books she'd acquired. All the stuff she could find about visions, dreams, prophecies, and so on. She had never read that much before, and it was getting somewhat frustrating. Although she'd found most of the books interesting, not one of them helped with her situation. The only useful thing was a bit about Pythia, where the author had suggested that the medium was under the influence when prophesying. At least, historically speaking, she now knew that she wasn't the only one, and that made Iris feel better.

Reclining on her couch, a secondhand copy of Dreams and Their Interpretation on her lap, she was trying to think about her future. After dumping Eddie, she had also quit her cleaning job — she couldn't concentrate on dirty windows and irritatingly heavy vacuum cleaners anymore. Her mind was constantly wandering elsewhere, and she felt she was actually living between two worlds at least.

Maybe she should talk with someone. The problem was that she didn't have many friends in Petersburg. Wanting to become an RnB star required some sacrifices, and the only people she'd kept in her inner circle were Eddie and Frankie, her childhood friend from Babylon, but they hadn't seen each other in ages, although she still had Frankie's phone number somewhere. She glanced sadly at the pile of demos crowding the upper part of her new shelf. Five years of sacrifice for what? No friends, no contract, no future. She reached for a joint she'd rolled earlier that morning. Eddie's stash was getting smaller and smaller.

The smoke in her lungs settled comfortably in its new home.

She had to concentrate more.

To be more focused.

She picked up the book, inhaled deeply from the joint, and watched the smoke swirl wildly above her head.

Exactly. Concentrate.

GOD SAYS:

UN PEU D'AIR SUR TERRE

Old Friends

THE AIR CONDITIONER buzzed continuously in the dark room, mingling with the various chaotic sounds coming from the street through the slits of the shutters—cars honking, radios blasting oriental music and the cries of the muezzins competing through loudspeakers, people arguing in violent outbursts, then laughing hysterically. If you listened carefully, you could hear the anguished murmur of the Mediterranean.

Hermes had always been partial to Alexandria, and the city hadn't changed over the centuries. It was an intricate maze, a living symbol of chaos, secrets, and mysteries. Wonderful. And an ugly city, too, to discourage those who weren't curious enough. Disappointment is often the first and the last door. He smiled, and Isis ran a smooth finger along his lips.

"What's on your mind?" she asked.

"You. This city. The future."

Isis turned around to pick up her cigarette, still burning on the night table.

"This city is the past," she said. "Or pasts, rather. Nothing will happen here."

Hermes looked at the beautiful goddess reclining next to him. Her breasts were small but perfect, her nipples pointing at the ceiling. He loved the color of her skin. It was too bad their lovemaking would be fruitless, but Jove's laws were still in force.

"What do you think will happen now?" she asked softly, blowing out curls of smoke.

Hermes shrugged, passing a quick hand through his hair.

"Who knows? Maybe nothing will happen. This is also a possibility. You know our ability to see the future is very limited. A few hours. A day at most. Only Pythia can see a little further than that—but not much further."

Isis reclined on one elbow, her right breast touching his arm.

"I wish things would change. I'm tired of waiting, pretending to be a singer, a movie star, a royal heir, or whatever. I'm tired of changing masks every century."

Hermes smiled. He felt like smoking a joint.

"Well at least you're alive. Some aren't back yet. Think of your husband."

Isis ran a slow finger across his chest, spreading needles of desire through his entire body. Under the sheets he felt himself grow harder, as she turned around to stub out her cigarette.

"He can rest some more. I'm fine for now."

Her mouth covered his and her tongue slid in, knowing exactly what it was looking for. Her perfume filled the darkness of his closed eyes. He welcomed her, not interrupting their kiss. With a swift, loving hand she guided him into her burning body.

"Do you really think they'll start building temples for us again?" she whispered in his ears as she slowly gyrated her hips, making his breath come in short gasps.

"If they don't, I will," he answered, pumping faster, keeping perfect time with her fantastic moves.

Smut in Alamut

THE SMELL OF incense was so pungent Iris almost threw up. Where was she now? She sure wasn't in her two-room apartment anymore. It looked like a medieval chamber, or something. A dungeon. Torches lit the place with their troubled light. There was a huge bed in the middle of the room, with a young man in a robe propped on an army of cushions, smoking a long, straight, and delicately-crafted wooden pipe. He was very handsome and very tanned. Taking a step closer, she realized he was an Arab youth, with bluish, acne-sprinkled cheeks, and she saw that what he was smoking wasn't just tobacco.

He took long drags, blowing out a haze of gray smoke that floated up to the ceiling. Iris watched him with some fascination. She noticed something protruding beneath the white djellabah — or whatever you called it — and she felt her loins warm up in spite of herself. The kid was handsome, sure, but mostly she hadn't had any sex for a good year, since her Rasta-head last loser boyfriend had run off with a banker — okay, the girl was cute and had great cocaine and he was nothing but a white loser, but still, she would kill her if she met her again.

She had never had sex with Eddie and never wanted to. Although their manager-future star relationship involved lots of power games, none of those were actually sexual. She had often wondered if Eddie was gay, but then, she hadn't felt anything for him either, so maybe by that way of thinking that made her a lesbian. But then there was the weird, moist feeling she had as this dark-skinned teenager sucked like a madman on his kif pipe.

The kid had turned gray now, his forehead covered with sweat. Iris thought he looked like he was about to throw up, and he actually heaved once or twice, pulling the pipe from his lips, but not letting go. It was like he was on a mission or something.

The door suddenly opened and an old man appeared, dressed entirely in black, with a tight round turban around his head. He looked like the Ayatollah Khomeini but with a sweeter face. He was escorted by ten men, bodyguards to judge by their armor and scimitars shining gloomily in the room's flickering torchlight.

"Hassan-i Sabbāh . . ." the young man murmured, obviously awed.

He tried to rise from his bed, but the old man lifted an appeasing hand and walked closer, followed by his henchmen. Iris knew his name. He was in one of the books she had read, about visions and hallucinations. He was the leader of the Hashishin, Islamic assassins who drugged recruits and showed them paradise before sending them on suicide missions. She felt a tingle of excitement run through her body. This was going to be good.

Hassan-i Sabbāh exchanged a few words with the young man, examining his eyes and taking his pulse. Nodding and smiling, he finally filled the pipe with a dark pellet, crushing it well under his thumb. Gesturing to one of the soldiers, he had him light the pipe and give it back to the young man, who thanked them.

Iris was frustrated. She regretted being a ghost in this scene, especially when the visitors had left the room. She wanted badly to try the pipe and eventually initiate the youth into unknown pleasures. But she knew there was nothing she could do, so she just kept staring, an impatient shadow standing in the dark.

The youth took a powerful hit from the pipe and weakened immediately. It must have been some powerful stuff. He fell back on the cushions, eyes showing white. He tried to raise the pipe once more, but his fingers opened and it fell on the ground with a sharp, dry knock.

As if it had been a signal, the door opened and the old man walked in again. He yapped a short order and the ten men lifted the sleeping youth from his couch. Another order and they left the room, shutting the door behind them.

After just a split second of hesitation she followed them, walking through the door like Casper the Friendly Ghost. After following a series of dimly lit corridors they arrived at a smaller, white-painted room with white furnishings. The large bed in the center, the chairs, the table — crowded with delicacies and bottles of many colors — were so white they hurt the eyes. A trio of white-clad musicians, with white instruments, played soft, whiny, hypnotic music.

The old man told his bodyguards to leave the boy on the bed. Then they retired, bowing their heads slightly as they left. Hassan-i Sabbāh locked the door and opened another, through which a string of scantily clad women entered. Their faces were covered by transparent veils and they had waist-length black hair. They wore golden metallic bikinis, decorated with coins. Hassan disappeared through the door, to reappear a few minutes later dressed in white babouches, djellaba, and turban. He sat on a high, throne-like seat facing the bed and barked an order to the women, who began carefully undressing the unconscious youth.

Iris admired the sizeable rod towering over the kid's stomach, with its all-powerful purple cap shining brightly in the candlelight. Another rapid command and two of the girls began to slowly lick the young man's cheeks.

He finally came to, looking around in surprise. His eyes were still red with kif and his movements were slow and awkward. He looked with disbelief at the old man, who nodded his assent. One of the girls kissed his mouth, while two others approached the erect member with theirs.

Iris felt like touching herself to relieve some of the erotic tension, but an awkward detail attracted her attention. One of the girls had hairy thighs. Sure, they were oiled and all, but still, she was an extremely hairy women. And her shoulders were large. Very large.

Iris stepped forward to take a closer look. The young man was in heaven, eyes closed, enjoying the sea of caresses crashing over his body. But these women weren't the promised virgins. Some had dark chins under the lipstick and the hands were strong and heavy. Men's hands. Their wigs weren't even on straight.

She backed away, slightly disturbed.

Meanwhile, Hassan-i Sabbāh's left paw had disappeared under his djellaba and was moving furiously up and down to the hypnotic rhythm of the music.

Publish and Perish

THE STRANGER SAT down opposite Sid. He was a large, Nordic-type man, with extremely piercing blue eyes, wearing a white suit with a half-open white shirt. A large silver cross, hanging from a long chain, spun above his stomach as he made himself comfortable in the chair. He was holding a dirty black duffle bag.

"What can I do for you then?" Sid asked, looking at his watch so that the Holy Water drinker would realize how busy he was.

"Well, I have a deal for you. A deal I don't think you can reject, considering the situation you're in."

Sid's thoughts galloped like a horse on crystal meth.

"What do you know about the situation I'm in?"

The stranger smiled.

"We know everything about page 261 and its dreadful consequences."

Sid felt cold sweat run between his shoulder blades.

"How the hell do you know about that? Did you have anything to do with it?"

The stranger smiled again. Exactly the same smile, as if he was a weird, blond machine with a strange, accented voice.

"Not directly, no. But indirectly, in a way, yes. Let's say we might have suggested the idea to someone who in his turn suggested it to someone else."

This guy is definitely mafia, Sid thought, but who the hell is he working for?

"Did Tonio send you? Is this part of the blackmail-me-into-oblivion-because-of-what-I-supposedly-did-to-his-daughter situation?"

The stranger laughed like a machine, rhythmically lifting his shoulders as he did so.

"No, and actually, you might want to turn on the television."

Sid's hand reached for the remote control, his eyes not deviating from the stranger's gaze. He was trans-fixed and, he didn't like it a bit, but there was nothing he could do: he felt as if he'd been transformed into a robot. He pressed the red button and immediately rec-ognized Tonio's house on the screen. It was on fire. The video was taken from a helicopter and Sid felt seasick from the motion. He searched for the volume button on the remote and pushed it up.

"There is no information about the origin of the explosion, but officials say that it doesn't appear to be mob-related. Some neighbors reported a strong odor of gas in the morning, which could be the explanation. Mobster Tonio Bronzino has perished in the accident, along with his daughter and two bodyguards. The bodies have been retrieved and were identified a few minutes ago . . ."

"That's the miracle you're talking about?"

"That's part of the miracle."

Sid was about to say something but the phone rang and he picked it up. It was the police. They were sorry, but they had bad news. Sid played along, feigning grief and despair until he put the receiver down. He scratched his cheek, thought about the situation for a second, and sighed.

"I get it. You blew up the house, I'm going to get the inheritance money and you want a part of the loot. Fair enough, although I don't really know what your motives were for wiping out my entire in-law family."

The visitor laughed silently. It was a weird, unexpected reaction.

"No. You won't get any money from them. Tonio locked you out of his will as soon as Maria told him she was divorcing you. All the money is going to charities. Catholic, of course."

Sid blanched.

"So I'm ruined?"

The man nodded with sadistic pleasure.

"Completely ruined."

After a spell of dizziness had passed, Sid felt a wave of anger shudder through him from the bottom of his soul.

"And that's a miracle?"

The stranger heaved the soiled duffle bag onto the table and opened it.

"No, this is the miracle. Fifty thousand dollars, small notes, random numbers. Real money too. And clean."

Sid blinked at the tens and twenties.

"For me?"

"For you."

"Is this a bribe? It's a little too much for vanity publishing."

"Not a bribe. An incentive. If you accept our deal, this will be added to the 50,000."

The man produced a check from a Bahamas Bank. Sid looked at the number one followed by a string of zeros dancing before his eyes.

"A million dollars," he whispered breathlessly. "Can this be real? Am I dreaming?"

The publisher caressed the cash in the bag with a trembling hand. The money felt real. He wasn't dreaming, and in a way that made things worse.

"Who sent you?"

"I told you before. Jesus sent me."

"Jesus?"

"Jesus."

"Jesus fucking Christ?"

"Jesus fucking Christ."

Sid's balding head was shiny with sweat now. He truly hoped Miss Jenkins wasn't listening to this. It was the craziest shit he had ever been involved in. A mob guy thinking he was some god-sent messenger. Yeah, sure. But the money was real. And right now, money was good.

"What does Jesus want me to do? Why are you here?"

"Ah," the man said and lifted a finger. "Hold on."

He rummaged in the duffle bag and took out a thick brown envelope, which he handed to Sid. 350 pages, circa, Sid thought, weighing it as he grabbed it.

"He wants you to publish this."

Sid peeked inside the envelope. It was a completely normal-looking manuscript in Times New Roman font.

"What is it?"

"The gospel according to Jesus."

Sid frowned.

"Hasn't this been published before? I mean, the New Testament and all that? I might be Jewish, but I have heard of it . . ."

The man shook his head. His eyes had regained their strange blue glow, as if a ball of electricity shone from behind them.

"No, no. Jesus actually wrote this. He finished it yesterday. The New Testament is pure Jove propaganda. Bullshit. This is the real McCoy. Straight from the source."

Sid took a deep breath. What he really needed now was a whisky.

"Why me?"

The stranger grinned.

"Isn't that what the Chosen all say?"

Sid removed the thick bundle from the envelope and skimmed through the first few pages.

"People are going to wonder. The Pope is going to wonder."

"Let them wonder. They will read it and understand."

A chapter title struck Sid.

"Destroy All Churches. Jesus never said that."

The man leaned back in the chair, joining his hands at chest level.

"Oh yes, he did. And many more things. You'd be surprised."

"How many copies?"

"We'll start with a million. In twelve languages."

Sid choked in disbelief.

"A million? But my printer could never do that much work! It'll take him years!"

"That's why we found you a printer who can."

The man took a business card from the breast pocket of his white jacket and handed it to Sid.

"Doomsday Printers. Never heard of them."

"They're waiting for you to give them the green light. Once you've edited the manuscript, that is."

"If Jesus really wrote this, I'm sure it's perfect. How can the Son of God make mistakes?"

"Well, English is not his native language. There might be a few words misspelled here and there. He's not sure his grammar is correct either."

"You know I publish porn and pulp fiction, don't you?"

"We do. We also know you have one of the best distribution networks in the market. Supermarkets, stations, airports, prisons, etc. Exactly what we need. With one of your catchy covers, this book is going to be the hit of the century. So, what do you say?"

Sid rubbed his chin a couple of times, feeling the sweat under his fingers. He wasn't dreaming and he wasn't dead — just talking to a fucking lunatic who was offering him a million dollars to publish some religious garbage.

"Well, Mr . . ."

"Gabriel. You can call me Gabe."

"Well, Gabe, do you have this on a CD-ROM or a flash drive?"

White Gloves and A Large Pair of Ears

Maria DaSilva was cooking the day's meal on her little gas stove in her tin, cardboard, and wood shack dead in the middle of Rio de Janeiro's largest favela, when she heard Flavio, her four-year-old son and only joy in life, softly cry for her.

What struck her immediately was that he wasn't calling in his usual voice. She had heard him call for her in many ways, out of hunger, fear, joy, and whatever other feelings a little boy can have so early in his life. Since his father had been killed by the police—by mistake, because he had never been associated with gangs, and she had many times regretted his honesty when she thought about the squalor they lived in—Flavio had been the center of his mother's hopes. She had enrolled him in a school run by foreigners who might have been communists but nonetheless gave the kids a sound basic education in the alphabet, numbers, and everything else they needed to begin a life that could eventually lead them out of this maze of misery and hopelessness.

So when she heard his anguished little squeal, she left the beans and pork to boil in the secondhand saucepan and ran into the other room, separated only by a sheet hanging on an old piece of string. When she saw what was standing in front of the TV, her first thought was that it was a joke, she later told the reporters.

Her heart almost stopped and her eyes took a moment to accept what they were seeing. Mickey Mouse® stood in the middle of the miserable room, hovering over Flavio, his hands dangling by his side, staring around as if he also was confused as to what was going on.

"He came out of the TV!" Flavio whined, running to his mother and pressing his face against her large stomach. "I was watching him and suddenly he came out!"

Mickey was neither very large nor very tall and Maria took courage. Telling her son to run to the local gang headquarters for reinforcements, she slowly moved toward Mickey. He didn't move, and she saw, with disbelief at first, that there was no trace of a zipper on his back. She felt him tremble slightly under her fingers and she retreated, not wanting to scare him more than necessary.

A few minutes later, her shack was filled with local mobsters and a large crowd of neighbors and onlookers, who had heard the incredible news. Mickey Mouse® waved silently at them, but didn't say a word. Some waved back, including Maria, Flavio, and Ernesto the gang leader. Nobody knew what to do. They just kept staring at each other in silence, until night fell and Mickey's unusually large ears threw huge shadows in the dim light.

"Creative Economics"

THE PETERSBURG TIMES: When Timothy Arden put his Golden VIP Deluxe credit card into the ATM at the corner of Grant Street and Bonaparte Avenue yesterday morning, he had no idea he would be one of the many victims of the greatest computer bug in the history of electronic banking systems.

He wanted to withdraw twenty dollars, but the machine refused. He was very surprised, as he knew he had received his yearly interest, which amounted to $126,000, from the Petersburg First Bank last Monday.

Cursing modern technology under his breath, he crossed the street to another ATM, where the same thing occurred. By now a little worried, he decided that it was probably a local network bug, and he walked a couple of blocks to where he knew a Petersburg First Bank office was located. When the ATM again rejected his card Arden said: "I asked for a receipt and looking at the paper I suddenly blanched and had to hold the wall for a few seconds to be sure I wasn't caught in a nightmare: somebody had emptied my account. Completely drained it. There wasn't a single cent left."

He rushed into the bank, where he had to join a long line of anguished customers yelling at the tellers and wanting to see the manager. After a long wait, he finally learned the appalling truth: somehow all bank accounts had been swapped with others. If Timothy Arden was ruined, someone else was very happy.

Although there have been rumors of a particularly vicious virus attack, authorities have released no information so far, only describing the chaos as a "major technical incident."

No one knows how long it is going to take to get this "bug" fixed, or what the economic impact might be. Optimists say that the impact on growth and consumption will be minimal, while pessimists assert that should this problem take too long to resolve it will prove more damaging than the crash of 1929.

Meanwhile, scenes of both violence and wild shopping sprees are reported across the country.

Viruses are a Language

STEENGO SMILED AND the admiral's scowl vanished; he was too smart and was a shining metal tube, now crackling and emitting an occasional alcoholic red nose, use our pop group instead. But it must be done—and the beast instantly opened its mouth—and those were tusks and tried to families?

What?

"Just in case we get blown away and you have to send in the second team?"

"Exactly. More questions?"

GOD SAYS:

A BOLD, HAUTE VICTORIAN RING MAKES
QUITE AN IMPRESSION

The Heavenly Corporation

HOLDING THE JOINT in her hand, Iris was nervous. She had smoked all of Eddie's stash and had gone to buy weed from her ex-boyfriend's dealer. The Rasta had promised it was the best she could get for the price, but then again, didn't they all say that? In any case, she was about to find out if it was true.

She had to understand before she could figure out what to do with her life. Understand what was happening to her every time she got stoned.

She lit the joint and inhaled deeply. The TV was turned on in the little room, glittering like a crazed stained-glass window. Music played in the background, some weird band she'd recently fallen in love with, called The Cyberpunk Candles, or whatever.

She would soon know if Eddie laced the stuff he was selling her. The rat. She would never talk to him again. Lousy as an agent, lousier as a friend. She inhaled and the smoke invaded her lungs, whirled inside, wrapped her in its harsh but delightful convolutions. So far, so good. She could still see the TV, feel the sofa under her butt, connect with the outside world. She began to relax.

Then suddenly she was standing in the middle of what seemed to be a hill covered with wheat, the grain so ripe it looked golden under the arching blue sky. A thin white cloud hung above the landscape, like a frozen plane. No more TV, room, or bookshelf.

So it wasn't Eddie's stash.

Definitely not.

She stood on a dusty path, naked as usual — although this didn't shock her anymore, she'd grown used to it by now. Not knowing what to do next, she followed the path until she noticed a small house in the distance, and outside was a man sitting in a rocking chair.

Walking closer, she could see he was an elderly black man, wearing shades and a '30s town hat. He was rocking slowly back and forth, humming a strange melody. It sounded like blues and yet it wasn't. His costume was pigeon-gray and absolutely clean, contrasting wildly with the shack. His hands, covered with large silver rings, clutched a cane with a silver pommel. He smiled as Iris approached.

John Lee Hooker, Iris thought. Now I'm having real strange visions.

"Well, well, well," he said, nodding. "What do we have here? Hermie was right. Things are cracking. What's your name, chile?"

The voice was soft and amused.

"Iris," she said. "What's yours?"

Although she had a hand cupped between her hips and an arm pressed against her breasts, she didn't feel threatened by the John Lee Hooker clone.

"You can call me Legba. Or Legs — that's fine by me, too."

Iris looked around, feeling a little lost. All the other scenes had been familiar somehow, but she couldn't remember anything from her religious history that resembled this one.

"Where am I? Who are you?"

The man laughed a deep, generous laugh. He sounded genuinely amused. Happy, even.

"Actually, I should be the one asking you questions. We don't get many visitors around here. At least not living ones. You're alive, aren't you, girl?"

Iris hesitated for a second, unsettled by the question.

"Yes. Well, I think so. I don't know."

"Can you see anybody else but me here?"

Iris shook her head.

"Then you're alive. Tell me, what are you doing here?"

Iris felt at a loss.

"Actually, I was counting on you to tell me."

The old man rocked silently, rubbing his chin.

"Hell, I don't know. Maybe you had an accident of some kind and you're floating. We do get floaters once in a while. But they sure don't look as real as you. And they're usually covered with blood."

"You mean this is Heaven?"

The man heard the distressed surprise in Iris's voice and chuckled.

"No, miss. This isn't Heaven. Nor Hell. Don't be alarmed. It's the Land of the Dead, that's all. No more, no less. What you see is what you get."

Iris looked around, helpless. Tears of self-pity rushed to her eyes and flowed down her cheeks. The stranger shook his head and tapped the cane gently, but firmly, between his feet.

"Relax, chile! I told you before: you're not dead. It's just a, hmmm, a channel problem. You shouldn't be here, that's all. You'll go back. In a little while. Like I told you, happens all the time. Cheer up, enjoy the company."

And the old man took a monster joint from his pocket and handed it to Iris.

Breaking News
Petersburg City Hall Sacked

REUTERS — ABOUT TEN thousand smokers, obese people, alcoholics, and drug addicts gathered today on Petersburg City Hall Plaza and stormed the official building, claiming that "banning smoking is fascism" and that they were going to return power "to those who really know how to enjoy life."

The demonstration appears to have taken security personnel completely by surprise, and they were unable to prevent the building being ransacked. Chief Robson, head of City Hall Plaza security, said: "These people were organized. They must have planned all this though the internet or something. We didn't see it coming."

The crowd is reported to have destroyed computers, furniture, and other city property. "It's lucky no one was hurt," said Sally Worth, a secretary who works on the twelfth floor. "These people ran amok."

It is believed that some city employees may have joined in the ransacking, but so far there has been no official confirmation of this.

The crowd is reported to have dispersed as quickly as it assembled, leaving officials puzzled.

"We're wondering if this is a one-off event or if it's the first of a series of such attacks and therefore something far more serious," said Commissioner Peterson. "We are investigating all possibilities and will leave no stone unturned in bringing these criminals to justice."

Many offices and much vital data, mostly concerning local taxes and ecological programs, were destroyed in the riot. Damage has been estimated at about two million dollars.

Liquor and tobacco companies, fast food chains, and organized crime have all denied any involvement in these events.

Publish and Perish

SID WAS CONTEMPLATING the Petersburg skyline through his window. Everything was going so well it seemed miraculous. The million books had been printed in no time, at the most ridiculously low cost he had ever heard of. The manager of the print works explained that Doomsday Books was in fact a charity and that was why they were so cheap. Hiring only brain-damaged and mentally handicapped personnel kept overheads down. Sid felt like Santa Claus with his elves. Idiots happily working for him. That, precisely.

The books sold themselves. He didn't even have to launch a publicity campaign. Two supermarket chains had already called to ask for repeat deliveries. The airport and central station too. First time it happened so fast.

He thought about the million bucks stashed in his safe and smiled, looking distantly at a promotion Zeppelin floating over the city. Why hadn't he thought about religion before? How could he have been so blind? Wasn't the Vatican the largest safe-deposit box in the world?

The answer was quite simple: he had never believed in God — for generations none of the Sapersteins had, not since his great-great-great-grandfather, a Rabbi, had been raped by a horde of Cossacks and left for dead. When he set foot in the New World he wasn't a Rabbi anymore. He was a professional gambler, with God is Hell tattooed in Yiddish across his chest.

There was a brief, dry knock on the door and Miss Jenkins walked in, wearing the red French ensemble he loved so much. He had given her a raise and their relationship had taken a new turn.

"I've got PCTV on the line. They want you on the Tabago Show tonight. What should I tell them?"

She was standing by the door, one hand on her hip and the other on the handle, her dark blonde hair pulled back in a bun, reading glasses on the tip of her nose. Her lips were slightly apart, in expectation of his answer. A collection of lascivious thoughts crowded the publisher's mind.

"Tell them: Hell, yeah. And come back right after. We've got some figures to check."

He winked at her and she got the message, winking back.

She closed the door and he heard her muffled voice say: "Hell, yeah."

That was his girl, all right.

Meanwhile

MEANWHILE, IN THE kingdom of France, absolutely nothing was happening.

GOD SAYS:

GET CHUCKED

The Heavenly Corporation

FRANKIE ARRIVED LATE, as usual. Iris's latte had turned cold and she ordered another one when the waitress strolled by to take another table's order. The Café Kropotkin was a brand new place, but had been designed in late nineteenth-century European style — or what the owners thought that style had been. To Iris it looked sinister, with dark red walls, framed paintings, distorting mirrors, tiny tables, and wooden chairs that squeaked when you moved. But it was the latest thing, and Frankie loved it.

Frankie was Iris's best friend, the only one who remained from their teenage Babylon high school clique. An old drughead like Iris herself, Frankie somehow managed to get decent grades that sent her to the Babylon College of the Arts, where she graduated in Media and Communication. After a stint at the Babylonian Vogue®, she moved to Petersburg and started her own fashion magazine, Sparkle®, which was a great success.

Of course, as with all important women in the fashion world, she was dressed in whatever had come to hand that morning—n'importe quoi—a light-brown leather jacket over a see-through black t-shirt with a multicolored ballerina skirt and pink cowboy boots. Following the stares that accompanied Frankie as she crossed the room, Iris hoped nobody would recognize her as the naked woman singing with all her hair sticking out on last month's Show Me Yours and I'll Show You Mine.

"Iris! It's been sooooo long!"

Bending over the table, Frankie hugged her friend so tight Iris stopped breathing. To feel squeezed by that iron grip made her feel a lot better and now she knew why she had called her old friend. As cracked in the head as she could be, Frankie had always been a terrific listener and a wonderful friend.

Frankie finally sat down, feeling her straight, long Heidi braids with the tips of her fingers. Her hair was dyed platinum blonde and Iris thought of putting on her sunglasses for a second.

Frankie ordered a Bloody Mary.

"It's past ten o'clock in the morning," she explained. "I can start drinking. I'm so glad you called! What's his name?"

Iris shot a faint smile and looked at her new latte.

"It's a little more complex than that, unfortunately."

Frankie giggled, stirring her blood-red drink.

"What can be more complicated than men? Money?

Is it money? You should have told me before—I would
have brought some cash."

Iris admired the way Frankie hadn't changed since
high school. A rich girl, she had always provided for
others. Beers, drugs, money—whatever one of the
clique had needed. Never a problem, eternal gratitude
never expected. "That's life," she used to say. "I was born
lucky, you weren't. Enjoy." She had also paid for Eileen's
abortion. Born lucky, yes. But more than that.

"Thanks, but it's not money. I work for a cleaning
company and it pays the bills."

"You're still a cleaning woman?"

Frankie sounded surprised, not shocked.

"I thought you were trying to make it as an RnB
singer? You have such a beautiful voice!"

Iris blushed and avoided Frankie's piercing eyes, she
felt relieved that Frankie had obviously not seen her
embarrassing five minutes of fame.

"Well, things happened. I'm not so sure now. But
that's not the problem either."

Before Frankie could play her guessing game again,
Iris grabbed both her hands and leaned closer, whispering.

"Frankie, I think I'm going insane."

"What?"

Not knowing where to start, Iris spat out the stories
of her visions in chaotic order. When she was finished,
Frankie stared at her, her Bloody Mary untouched.

"Wow! That sure is something. You mean you smoke

a joint and bam! You're with Moses . . ."

Iris nodded.

"Exactly. And it's driving me insane. Scares the shit out of me. I don't know what to do."

Frankie finally took a long sip of her cocktail, making a long sucking noise that drew some attention—again.

"Why don't you stop smoking pot?"

"Yes," Iris said feebly.

She actually hadn't thought about that. Could it really be that simple?

"But what about the vision I had with Eddie? It was so vivid?"

Frankie frowned, played with her straw.

"Can you try it with me?"

"Here?"

"Sure, who cares? Might get you some publicity."

Iris glanced nervously around. She hadn't been shy before. After all, she'd sung naked live. But this was different. It was as if she was naked again, but in a different way.

"Okay, give me your hands."

She grabbed Frankie's fingers and closed her eyes. She felt an incredible rush, like a massive gust of wind engulfing her face, forming a silver tunnel. At the end of the tunnel, like on an old TV set, she saw Frankie wake up and grab a small mirror smudged with a rest of cocaine. Frankie licked it conscientiously, until the silvery surface was glittery clean. The image disappeared and Iris found herself staring right at Frankie's face again.

"So? Did you see anything?"

Iris whispered in her ear what she had seen. Frankie's eyes widened.

"Oh my God—this is so embarrassing! You won't tell anyone, will you?"

Iris shook her head, feeling uncomfortable.

"You have a real talent there, you know that, girl? Can you see anything in the future?"

Iris shook her head again.

"No, it's always the past. Not good for anything, I guess."

"Do you know how to read Tarot cards?"

Iris thought about all the books on her shelves. Maybe they weren't a waste of money after all.

"I've never tried, but I think I could, yes."

"Listen, I'm throwing a little party Saturday night . . . Why don't you come as a special guest, with a Tarot deck? I'll put you up in a corner, by the swimming pool, and you can tell people's fortunes for twenty dollars a pop. I'm sure you can make a lot of money with that talent of yours!"

"But, Frankie, I can't see the future!"

Frankie laughed, long and beautifully.

"If you can tell people about their past, darling, they'll believe anything you say about their future!"

Slow Tornado

AP — THE VIDEO, taken with a mobile phone, is shaky and blurred. It shows a tornado nearing an interstate. A farm standing in its path is soon blown to pieces. Shards of wood, tiles, and pieces of furniture appear and disappear in the whirlwind, like ornaments on a twisting Christmas tree. Everything seems to be happening in slow motion—except for a few cars passing by on the interstate at top speed—as if the tornado is advancing at an incredibly low speed. The tornado keeps moving extremely slowly, as do the objects trapped within it. A voice repeats: "I can't believe this, I can't believe this!"

The video was first shown on YouTube, then on various TV channels. There are no indications regarding the date or location of the phenomenon and so far no one has been able to determine whether it is an elaborate hoax.

Old Friends

THE TEMPERATURE DROPPED drastically as Hermes stepped into the darkness of the open garage. The 1959 Oldsmobile glowed faintly and smelled of fresh paint. It was a cream-colored convertible with bright red seats. A beautiful job. Hermes noticed a small signature, under the right side chromed rear mirror—a blue lightning bolt. He remembered the sign over the garage. Thunderbird's Custom Shop. Of course, what else?

A back door opened and Thunderbird himself walked in, wiping his grease-stained hands with an already soiled handkerchief.

"Hermie!" He smiled, noticing the visitor. "What brings you to Utah? You become a Mormon?"

"Not a chance. Beautiful car."

Thunderbird grinned, his Indian features parching up like the desert under the baking sun.

"You want to try it?"

Hermes smiled.

"Isn't it for sale?"

"Actually, it's sold already. But I haven't tried it myself yet. New engine, brakes, automatic gear, whatever. Hop in. Watch out for the paint, it might not be dry yet. I don't want to buy you a new suit. Armani?"

"Yves Saint Laurent."

"Whatever."

Hermes found himself comfortably seated behind the Bakelite steering wheel.

"Brings back lots of memories," he sighed.

"Like what?"

Thunderbird had joined him, sunglasses over his hooked nose.

"Vegas, 1962."

"Ah, yes."

They both smiled at the same time.

"Sinatra."

"Sinatra."

Hermes drove out of the garage, into Scottsville's main street. The engine purred beautifully.

"You've done an amazing job. So, it is sold already?"

Thunderbird nodded.

"Over the Net. The guy actually should come by later today."

"How much?"

"Ten thousand."

"That's cheap."

"That's sold."

They drove out of town. Thunderbird had turned on the radio and country music rippled the air between them.

"So what brings you to these parts, friend? You come far?"

Hermes smiled, keeping his eyes on the road. It was almost deserted. Just a pick-up truck, once in a while.

"You heard the news, right?"

Thunderbird nodded.

"Who hasn't? Are the signs confirmed?"

Hermes shrugged.

"We're working on it. A lot of activity is going on. Pythia is formal."

"Still the one, hey?"

"Still the one."

Hermes set the cruise control at seventy. He took a joint from his breast pocket and handed it to Thunderbird, who lit it with the car's lighter.

"Peace pipe good."

They laughed.

"You heard they're banning tobacco everywhere?" Thunderbird resumed. "We gave tobacco to men. They're banning it and we're coming back."

He shook his head.

"About time this bad craziness stopped. Can't wait. Here, have a hit."

Hermes took a drag, relaxing.

"What's the news from your side?"

The God of Thunder and Messenger of the Gods shrugged.

"People are getting excited. It's hard for some to hold their horses, but we don't want to fuck everything up a second time. One Thanksgiving is enough in history."

Hermes nodded and passed Thunderbird the joint.

"Pythia says there's more to come. We must wait. Be patient."

"Patient? Hell, give me a good vintage car to customize and I can wait forever. Best thing the white man ever invented."

"That and the Apocalypse," Hermes grinned.

"That and the Apocalypse," Thunderbird confirmed.

Laughing, the Thunder God smoked the last bit of weed and let the butt fly over his head, a tiny white butterfly amidst the yellow hills and enormous blue sky.

GOD SAYS:

WITH EVERY STEP
WITH EVERY STONE
LOVE GROWS

Publish and Perish

IT WAS THE first time Sid had been invited to a TV show and his excitement was spiked with disappointment. He had imagined a glamorous studio with lots of lights and whatnots, but here he was, confined to a tiny cell, with an overweight makeup artist by the name of Ferdinand who was making him choke under layers and layers of foundation. No champagne, not even a gin and tonic. Sparkling water or soda. Fuck that shit! Where was the red carpet? After all, the goddamned book had sold over 700,000 copies in the first six months. An absolute hit. And fifty-four countries had asked for translation rights, including China!

"Don't move," Ferdinand said. "You don't want your face to catch unwanted light."

Sid thought about his ex-wife and Tonio. Losers. He sneered and Ferdinand scolded him again. They thought they could screw him—but who's sorry now? Must be so pissed off on their little clouds. And Marco too, wherever he might be. Actually, he should try to find him and thank him for that missing page. Destiny. He inhaled deeply with satisfaction.

There was a brief knock on the door and Miss Jenkins walked in, followed by Gabe.

"You're on in five minutes."

Ferdinand gasped and rummaged among his pencils.

Miss Jenkins bent over and gave Sid a quick kiss on the lips.

"It's a pleasure working for you, Sid."

"Don't worry, you'll get your raise."

"Always the romantic."

"Always."

She waved goodbye as she closed the door. Gabe, who'd stayed in the room, picked up and opened a can of soda.

"Are you ready for this?" he asked before taking a long gulp.

Sid shrugged.

"Sure. Why do you ask?"

Gabe looked him directly in the eyes, smiling.

"Because things might become suddenly dangerous."

Ferdinand squeaked.

"How do you mean?" Sid asked, a little uneasily.

Gabe finished his soda and crushed the can in his hand.

"We have information that your book pissed some people off. Important people."

"Publishers? Fuck 'em."

Gabe straightened himself up, looking for dust on his jacket.

"No, not publishers. People with a lot more power. But you shouldn't be alarmed. We're watching out for you."

"Thanks."

Sid felt ridiculous, but what else could he say. He could understand that people were mad at him. The book was a religious time-bomb and it sold like crazy. He was glad he wasn't a Muslim. He would probably be dead by now. Or living in a seedy motel, dressed up as a woman, in some witness protection program.

"I'll be careful," he added, winking at his protector.

Gabe gave a thumbs-up and left the room.

Sid felt a cold sweat run down his spine, but he wasn't scared. Just terribly angry that anyone would want to take his fortune from him. Let them show their ugly snouts, he thought, as Ferdinand was giving him a final touch up, and they'll see who they're dealing with.

Tabago's assistant—a beautiful, itsy-bitsy model of a woman who looked like Louise Brooks with red hair—walked in and signaled. It was time.

Thanking Ferdinand for his *travail*, Sid followed the tiny woman down a corridor crowded with electrical equipment. His heart was beating slightly faster than usual, but he wouldn't admit it was because he was nervous.

That coffee was terrible, he thought instead. *Why can't they get a decent brand, with all those commercials?*

The spotlights nearly blinded him and he screwed up his eyes and looked at the set through tightened eyelids. That shadow over there was probably Tabago. The mini Louise Brooks stopped and showed him the way. He walked in to thunderous applause. Finally, he thought, *the real thing*.

Spontaneous Combustions

AP — A SERIES of unexplained incidents is alarming the media, artistic, and literary worlds: in the past week, five celebrities have become victims of what are claimed to be the first ever well-documented cases of spontaneous human combustion.

The first victim, Michael Sportis, the well-known lead singer of the MTV-nominated band Blood and Breadsticks, was leaving the famous Petersburg club, La Folie, when his head suddenly burst into flames and the rest of his body quickly ignited. His girlfriend, Tania, was slightly injured.

The following morning, Kyra Henderson, the award-winning actress from In Your Bed, Out of Your Head, was standing in line in a Hollywood Starbucks when her coat caught fire and she was engulfed in seconds. Although there was suspicion of a criminal act, surveillance cameras showed that no one in the shop had actually approached or attacked the star.

Later the same day, Denis Gouraud, the famous French philosopher and author of the bestseller, To Live is to Think, was sitting at a café table in Paris for a press interview when flames shot from the top of his head and the fire spread to his entire body in a few seconds. The interviewing journalist was taken to the hospital suffering from shock.

On Wednesday afternoon, concept artist Werner Stück was presenting his latest creation, a pile of dusty brooms stained with paint which he said represented the "carelessness of our modern world," when his left hand was suddenly enveloped in flame. Before anyone could react the artist was reduced to cinders. Authorities at first thought the cause was a freak accident in which a cigarette made contact with a nylon shirt, but witnesses said that Stück wasn't smoking and that, furthermore, he was wearing a black cotton shirt.

Finally, in what appears to be the most dramatic occurrence in this ghastly series of events, anchorwoman Betty Chong of BTV News literally exploded into flames as she was presenting the candidates for next September's elections. The tragedy happened live, sending millions of viewers into shock.

Although none of these mysterious cases seem to be related, many religious figures have claimed that they are a divine warning against "decadence, profit, and amorality." Scientists and experts admit being unable to explain these events and have called a special conference in Paris to set up a research agenda.

Le Café Jaune

REUTERS — A MAN claiming to be Vincent van Gogh was arrested yesterday in Arles, France. The man, said by a waitresses to bear a "striking resemblance" to the renowned painter, sat down on the terrace of the famous Le Café Jaune, featured in van Gogh's masterpiece Café Terrace at Night. "He looked agitated and strange," said M. Sanchez the Café's manager. "It was a little past five in the evening and we had many customers in for aperitifs."

Apparently dissatisfied with the service, the man insulted a waitress and demanded her attention. He then ordered absinth, a type of alcohol banned in France since 1915. The waitress explained that absinth was illegal, but instead of changing his order the man insisted, saying it was a scandal and accusing her of not serving him because he was Dutch.

The manager tried to calm the man down to no avail. He is reported to have become increasingly agitated, threatened other customers, and shouted religious imprecations. The manager finally called the police, who arrested the man after a brief scuffle.

Questions remain about the man's identity and motives. When searched, he had no ID and his only money consisted of two valueless 1887 Franc coins. He was carrying a small notebook containing ink sketches of the city, drawn in Van Gogh's style and apparently so well executed that, according to one source, they could "baffle" experts. When asked to sign his statement, the man simply wrote "Vincent."

He was taken to a local psychiatric hospital, where he continues to claim to be Vincent van Gogh and has asked for artists' materials to be brought to his cell.

A photograph of the man will be issued to the media in the coming days in the hope that friends and relatives will come forward and identify him.

The Heavenly Corporation

FRANKIE HAD REALLY outdone herself for her party. Her apartment had been repainted with Mondrian motifs, little squares and rectangles in the three basic colors, with matching furniture. It was more than decoration, it was an experience in itself—especially with Frankie standing in the middle of it all, in a vintage '60s dress with a Mondrianesque print and thigh-high white vinyl boots.

Sitting at her assigned table by the pool, Iris was both excited and resentful. The party had started about an hour ago and was going full blast, her ears were hurting from the music, gossip, and hysterical bursts of laughter from guests acknowledging one another. So far she hadn't had a single "customer"—she didn't know what to call them—and her hands, mechanically playing with the cards, were moist and sticky. She hoped nobody would want to shake hands, but then again, why would anybody do that?

She ordered her third strawberry Daiquiri from a cute Indian waiter whose very dark eyes eerily reflected the movements of the pool's surface. Then a thin-boned, nervous-looking young man sat in the chair facing her, a half mocking, half uneasy smile shaping the lower part of his face. An older woman stood behind him, reassuringly massaging his left shoulder with one hand and nursing a nearly finished scotch on the rocks in the other.

"Frankie told me you had real talent," the young man whispered, so quietly Iris had to lip-read half the sentence. "How do I know that?"

A feeling of cold anger and desperation rose in her, making her feel even more like a con artist than when she'd set up the table earlier in the afternoon, listening to all of Frankie's recommendations. She felt she should just end the masquerade right now, stand up, flip the table over, and throw the cards into the pool in a dramatic storm of cardboard and colors, but she chose to give the smartass her most mysterious smile.

"Here, give me your hands."

She entwined her fingers in his. They were surprisingly cold. She held back a shiver and closed her eyes. There was a flash of painful white light and there he was. Standing in his bathroom, bare-chested and finishing a shave. He sprinkled water over his face and rubbed his cheeks vigorously before looking at himself in the mirror. Satisfied, he reached for the watch resting on a glass shelf above the basin. He miscalculated and knocked the watch—an expensive gold thing—directly into the open toilet. Cursing, he knelt down and plunged his hand into the water to retrieve it.

When she opened her eyes, she saw that it was the same watch he now wore around his wrist. In a flat, matter-of-fact, professional tone, she described to him what she had seen. His jaw dropped and he attempted to conceal the watch. He told her that she was incredible.

She drew the cards for him, trying to remember every nuance that could be gleaned from the symbols. She'd studied her Tarot carefully over the last couple of days, going through the major and minor arcana again and again. When she realized she would never master the minor ones—there were 56!—she decided to stick to the 22 major ones. And even that proved difficult. But she had no choice now—it was either do her best or go back to cleaning the apartments of Petersburg's rich for the rest of her life.

She looked at the cards and told the young man what she could remember about them, improvising about half of it. When she'd finished he stared at her for a couple of seconds, then shook his head, while taking a wad of bills from his pocket.

"Wow! You are amazing! Do you have a card? I'd love to consult you again, if it's okay with you. And I'm going to tell all my friends about you!"

Iris thanked him, secretly relieved that it had gone so well, and took the bills. There was an extra twenty. So far, so good, she thought. But it only got better. Twenty-five minutes later, guests were queuing around the pool to consult her.

GOD SAYS:

MY RUNNING PARTNER AND I HAVE NEVER MET

A Rose is a Rose

DISORIENTED, BACHIR STOPPED his camel. He was sure he wasn't suffering from sunstroke and he hadn't used kif for the last couple of days. Also, he knew this part of the desert like the back of his hand—as a Bedouin, he was born with the sharp-backed dunes in his blood. Nonetheless, he took a quick look at his GPS system, which confirmed his fears: he wasn't lost at all. As the oldest, the tribe had sent him ahead to the oasis to see if any other caravans were out here. He had taken this same three-day route many times before.

At first he thought it could have been the Israelis—one of their farms or Kibbutzim—a new plantation or something like that. They did that in some parts of the desert, but they had never done it here. Not in the middle of nowhere. What was more, there weren't any buildings around, or men or cattle or anything. Just this strange patch of green grass, shining softly under the harsh sun.

To make sure he didn't have sunstroke, Bachir made his camel kneel down and carefully dismounted. Grabbing the AK-47 from the side of the animal, he took a few steps, then crouched, extending a curious hand. Yes, it was grass and it was slightly moist. He rolled his fingers to feel the dampness and an unbelieving smile flashed across his face. His eyes wandered over the uneven surface until they found a small clump of flowers growing in the grass. They were small, yellow roses and their heads shimmered in the warm air. He had seen some of these flowers before, at markets in Israel, wrapped in cellophane cones and sold by recent immigrants.

He felt their hard stems and stroked their beautiful petals. He wanted to pluck them and take them back to his wife and show them to the tribe. But he resisted the temptation, whispered a prayer to Allah, and climbed back on his camel. Such beauty had to be left untouched. He felt lucky he'd been able to witness it. And he knew he wouldn't tell anyone. The djinns didn't like their secrets to be known, and he didn't want to die. He would lie to the others about this place, so that no one would ever find it—and he would even try to erase it from his memory, at least until he had grandchildren. Then he could tell this true story that would one day become a legend.

Publish and Perish

TABAGO'S WHEELCHAIR SHONE under the spotlights and hurt Sid's eyes. Why hadn't he thought of sunglasses? He was waiting for Tabago to finish presenting the book and cracking his little jokes, making the audience laugh on cue. The TV star finally turned his chair toward him and they exchanged polite commercial smiles.

"Well, Mr. Saperstein, you know why we invited you tonight."

Sid was about to answer, but Tabago didn't give him time.

"Because the author was impossible to reach!"

A burst of cheers and laughter came from the invisible audience.

"So, you really think this book was written by the Jesus Christ?"

Sid briefly glanced at Gabe's inscrutable face, sitting in the first row of the audience. He was wearing sunglasses. Smart kid.

"Yes, absolutely. I wouldn't have published it otherwise."

There was a programmed murmur of disbelief from the darkness on the other side of the spotlights.

"How did you get your hands on the manuscript? Did the Lord walk into your office and say, 'Publish this or you'll burn in Hell'?"

Laughter. Applause.

"Well, almost. Of course I can't reveal what happened, but let's say that someone gave me the manuscript. Someone the Lord could trust."

"And someone who is probably very, very old!"

Tabago waited for the laughter to subside, an electric smile pasted across his professionally smirking face.

"Now, I have a question . . . How can we be sure Jesus Christ really wrote this neo-New Testament? (Laughter) There are a number of surprising things in it . . . I quote: 'Do not build churches in my name. To follow purity is to follow a sinful path. Charity is another name for oppression . . .' What does the Pope think of all this?"

Sid wiped his forehead with the white handkerchief Miss Jenkins had given him earlier that morning. It still smelled of her perfume and it made him feel better.

"Well, he hasn't called me yet," he said, smiling. "But these are the true words of Christ, believe me. If you've read the book, you'll understand. If you haven't read it yet, you will."

Sid suddenly felt very strange, as if someone was using him as a glove puppet.

"Have you read the book, Mr. Tabago?"

The entertainer squirmed on his chair.

"Well, I . . . My assistant . . . Whom I trust . . ."

Silence fell on the audience.

"I don't have time to read everything, you see . . . But . . . But . . . What's going on?"

Tabago looked at Sid with panic-filled eyes, but the publisher couldn't move. He was locked in his chair, a wonderful, warm smile pasted across his face.

Not a good time to panic, he thought, and he hung tight as Tabago slapped his thighs with cries of surprise.

"I can feel my legs . . . I can feel . . . It's like . . ."

There was a mounting murmur of disbelief as the entertainer slowly rose from his chair, his whole body shaking.

"It's incredible . . . I can . . . I can walk!"

He took a few steps, a hand resting on his desk, just in case.

"I can walk!"

Tabago lifted his arms into the air and Sid felt a flash of incredible heat pierce his body, then he watched in horror as the entertainer collapsed on the ground, holding his chest.

"Allelu . . ." Tabago began, then clenched his jaws, closed his eyes and died.

After a few seconds of astonished silence, panic seized the studio and the screaming audience stampeded toward the exit gates as the crew rushed on stage, followed by medics and onlookers. Sid felt a heavy hand grab his shoulder and he exhaled noisily, as if he'd been swimming underwater for too long.

"Let's go," Gabe said, helping Sid off the couch. "Things are getting complicated."

Old Friends

SITTING ON AN ammo box in this Central American jungle, Hermes remembered how much he hated nature. An insect zoomed by his head, and he slapped his cheek. He didn't even really know where he was. Mexico? Guatemala? Nicaragua? As the God of Roads and Crossroads, there was definitely some irony in that.

A beautiful young woman appeared in the tent, wearing fatigues and a cap pulled down to her eyebrows. She was obviously Indian, and her dark, slanted eyes were mesmerizing. A hundred centuries earlier, Hermes thought, and anything could have happened.

"El Comandante will be here in a minute," she said. "He apologizes for keeping you waiting. Is there anything I can do for you?"

"No, gracias. I'll be fine."

The woman disappeared and Hermes looked around his friend's HQ. Ammo boxes, an old door used as a desk covered with tons of maps and papers, a power generator, and a bookshelf crammed with paperbacks.

The Greek god got up from his seat, careful not to stain his brand new Banana Republic suit, and knelt in front of the shelf, letting his eyes run along the colorful covers.

"History books," a familiar voice said behind him. "Most of them, at least."

Hermes stood up, turned around.

"Good to see you, Tez."

"One can learn a lot of things from human history. It's also our history, in a way. Glad to see you, too, Hermie. What brings you to our savage parts?"

Tezcatlipoca, the Aztec God of War and the Protector of Sleeping Children, hadn't changed since the last time Hermes had seen him, in another jungle, in the early '60s. Round-faced, a friendly smile constantly floating around his lips, his eyes were the only frightening feature about him—cosmic-black, they seemed to steal the light and never send it back.

"Haven't you heard the news?" Hermes asked, a little confused and thought: How can anyone live in such isolation?

Tezcatlipoca laughed earnestly.

"Of course, I heard. What do you think? That in this jungle we are cut off from civilization?"

Hermes thought, yes, but kept it to himself. Tezcatlipoca made him nervous, as all the Old Rites gods did. He found them savage and unpredictable. Barbarians.

"No, not at all. I was just wondering. I came to hear your opinion on the matter."

Tezcatlipoca shrugged and reached for a cigar in the breast pocket of his fatigues. Hermes thought about all the ammo in the tent, but guessed Tez knew what he was doing.

"I don't know. We've been through this before. Hell, our people thought the Spaniards were gods! I wonder if we're making the same mistake."

Hermes nodded.

"Yes, that's always a possibility. But Pythia is certain."

Tezcatlipoca lit his cigar with a Zippo and, closing his eyes, took a long drag.

"I heard about that too. Sure is convincing. But tell me, honestly, Hermie, if that's true, if freedom—our freedom, that is—is at hand, do you think we're ready for it?"

Hermes thought about old stories chock-full of gods and humans. Friends, lovers, enemies, suckers, whatever. His heart swelled.

"Yes, absolutely."

Tezcatlipoca shook his head behind the blue cloud.

"Things have changed so much. Centuries have passed. Human sacrifices are out of fashion. I mean, in the old ways. There are some things we can never go back to. I know that, and you know that. We have to reinvent everything, in a way. And they do too. Humans, I mean. Mortals. When they realize that they're free, that the world is free, will they want us back? Will there still be room for us?"

"Mortals are children, Tez. They need us. They always have, they've kept us alive by hiding us, changed our names and symbols so that we'd go unnoticed. Why should that change?"

Tezcatlipoca sat down in his folding chair, half reclining.

"I don't know if it'll change, I agree, Hermie. But after all these years, fighting like I did side by side with them, right here, in these jungles, I kind of hope it will. For them."

"You know that it'll be chaos, without us."

Tezcatlipoca smiled distantly.

"Shouldn't we give them the chance? At least once?"

Hermes suddenly felt uneasy.

"And what about us? What would become of us?"

Tezcatlipoca blew out a cloud of blue cigar smoke. His eyes were even blacker than before.

"You have lived in comfort for too long, you and your civilized friends. Even your own freedom scares you now."

Coming out of the tent, Hermes gasped for air. That was all he needed: one of the major gods gone completely insane.

Total–Death Experience

AFP — A LARGE-SCALE tragedy occurred today in Milan when during a Near-Death Experience conference, attended by more than 114 specialists from around the world, the concrete roof of the conference hall collapsed on the audience. According to the authorities, although help arrived swiftly on the scene, there were no survivors.

Chemicalia

REUTERS — ACCORDING TO a recent article published in Nature, a common enzyme found in dishwashing detergent could be one of the most powerful drugs ever invented.

The enzyme was thought to be harmless until recent tests on rats showed that at a high dosage the chemical triggered strong psychotic reactions, comparable to those caused by powerful drugs like datura, LSD, or yage. Hallucinations related to these drugs are often so real that it is impossible for users to know whether or not they are functioning normally.

"We don't know how the enzyme actually reacts with the human body. Maybe it disappears, maybe it stays hidden, leading to effects close to those of lead poisoning. What happened with the rats is not necessarily what happens to humans," said Mr. Moto, the researcher. "But still, over twenty years we absorb about a kilogram of it, which is ten thousand times more than we've given the rats. So the question remains open."

Publish or Perish

"WHAT'S GOING ON?" Sid asked Gabe, as the man escorted the publisher and Miss Jenkins to his car in the building's parking lot.

"Get in!" Gabe said, opening the door for them.

"No!" Sid protested. "Not before you tell me what's going on! What was that all about?"

Gabe frowned, looking around nervously. Sid had never seen him like this. Miss Jenkins stood between them, hesitating.

"Sid, maybe we should . . ."

"No!" The publisher yelled. "I know something happened back there and that our friend here is scared. Why?"

Miss Jenkins looked at Gabe. It was true the Aryan looked uneasy.

"Please," Gabe started, "I'll explain. But not now."

"Yes, now!"

There was a sudden flash of light and an incredi-

ble burst of heat followed by a short scream and the
stomach-churning smell of burnt chicken skin. Before
Sid could register what he'd seen—namely a completely
combusted Miss Jenkins crumpling to the ground—
Gabe had seized him by the arm, pushed him inside
the car, jumped into the driver's seat and driven off at
high speed.

Sid was in shock, remaining completely silent as he
swayed with the car around the tight curves, ears smart-
ing from the screeching of the tires. It was only when
the car emerged into full daylight, zigzagging through
the traffic, that the publisher was able to speak again.

"Gabe," he said. "I think I'm going to throw up and
pass out."

And that's exactly what he did.

GOD SAYS:

INFUSIUM 23 BRINGS YOU A LINE OF SPECIALIZED SOLUTIONS THAT HELP KEEP YOUR PROBLEM HAIR UNDER CONTROL. ITS i23 ESSENTIAL TREATMENT COMPLEX ENHANCES THE TEXTURE AND CONDITION OF YOUR HAIR, PROVING THAT SCIENCE CAN BE A BEAUTIFUL THING.

Riding the Underground

AFP — PASSENGERS ON Line 1 of the Paris Metro were shocked today when an 1890s train arrived instead of the usual, modern one.

"It was incredible," said Sofie-Anne Peyronnet, a 35-year-old schoolteacher. "It was like being at Euro Disney, with those shiny, wooden cars. The lights especially were strange. Very yellow."

What was even more strange for the passengers was when someone in the front car realized that nobody was driving the train.

"I freaked out," explained Gérald Bronner, a 42-year-old sociologist. "All of a sudden it wasn't fun anymore. It was scary."

However, the train stopped normally at the next station, and alarmed passengers disembarked on the platform and watched the train disappear into the tunnel.

A spokesperson for the Paris Metro said they had no knowledge of an 1890s train being used on Line 1 and

suggested that the passengers may have experienced a
shared hallucination.

The Heavenly Corporation

IT WAS THREE in the afternoon and the Café Kropotkin was practically deserted. That was why Frankie and Iris had made it their regular Tuesday meeting place. Today it was Iris's turn to be late—a last minute séance with an up-and-still-coming actor she couldn't say no to. She apologized to Frankie, who— dressed in nothing but black vinyl—looked stunning.

"No problem," said the Fashion Queen. "I'm so glad it's all going so well for you!"

"I owe you everything," Iris replied, making herself comfortable on the fin-de-siècle chair. "If you hadn't invited me to your party eight months ago none of this would've happened. Who could have predicted?"

"Well—you. At least you should have."

They laughed and Iris ordered her sparkling water. Since her business had picked up, she felt she should be more careful with her looks. She ate only salads and drank only water, except at cocktail parties, where she munched on everything she could get her hands on and drank as many glasses of champagne as she could—before making a complete fool of herself. Fortunately for her weight and reputation, such parties only occurred every two weeks or so.

"But couldn't. Can't." Iris said, with some resentment.

She smirked.

"You know I'm a fraud."

Iris had whispered, but Frankie snapped her fingers, looking angry.

"Don't say that! Someone might hear you. Besides, a lot of my friends told me you were right on the money."

Iris took a sip, enjoying the fizz of the bubbles on her tongue.

"Sheer luck," she said again. "But don't worry, I'm loving every minute of it. And it's great to have you as an agent."

"Friend." Frankie protested. "Speaking of which, I'm really angry with Tabago for letting us down like that! I'd just got you booked for the following week. A god-damned miracle—and he croaks right in the middle of it! Did you watch the show?"

Iris shook her head.

"No, but I saw it on the news. Unbelievable. Was he really paralyzed?"

Frankie shrugged and waved to the waiter for a second round.

"Yeah, I think he was a real cripple. Never saw him without his chair. It shocked me so much I bought the book he was talking about. The new Bible, or whatever."

"So?"

"I haven't opened it yet. Just bought it. I'm planning to read it when I retire. Next week."

They both laughed and Frankie blew a lock of hair away from her left eye.

"Anyway, darling, let's quit the shop talk. How's your love life? What happened to Max Walcroft, tennis-man extraordinaire?"

"Eliminated in the semifinals. He was a jerk."

Frankie bit her lower lip.

"Oh, no. I'm sorry."

"Don't be. His backhand was terrible."

They laughed and raised their glasses.

"To us girls," Frankie said.

"To us."

The clinking of their glasses as they toasted each other resounded in the dark and empty café like a strange child's laughter.

Mommy, Look What I've Drawn!

CURSING UNDER HER breath because she was going to be late for work, Debbie Parsons put on her jacket as she walked down the hallway and then remembered she hadn't turned off the coffee machine.

Surrounded by the strong smell of morning, she trotted back to the counter and was about to switch off the glowing red button when her eye caught a small silhouette walking past her window.

Her heart skipped a beat, like it did every time she spotted a little girl who reminded her of Lauren. The pain had faded over the years—she was amazed at the human capacity to survive tragedy—but there was still that painful reflex every now and then. She knew John had it too, they'd often talked about it, as they had about adopting or not adopting—finally agreeing on the latter.

It was strange for Debbie to keep noticing similarities between unknown children and her own poor dead Lauren, as she and John had completely changed their lives after the accident, selling the house, moving to another city, starting over. Nothing here could remind her of Petersburg or anything about her life there, and yet all it took was a little girl in a duffle coat to send her spinning back into her own pain.

Shrugging, Debbie pressed the "off" button on the coffee machine and zipped up her jacket. When she reached the corridor, she was startled by the sound of the doorbell. Shit, she thought, the postman, or some idiot selling things. No time now.

She opened the door and didn't see anybody at first. Puzzled, she took a step back and then froze. The little girl she'd seen through her window was standing in front of her, a woolen cap set low over her eyes and her face half hidden by her misty breath. Although the chill of the morning made her eyes water, Debbie couldn't help noticing the girl's uncanny resemblance to Lauren, and she felt a pang of sadness in her chest.

The little girl, saying nothing, offered Debbie something white. It was a drawing. Exactly the same kind of drawing Lauren used to do. A princess, a palace, and a horse. She couldn't believe her eyes and she felt her knees grow weak. It was even signed Lauren in an uneven hand on the upper right corner.

Debbie's puzzlement gave way to anger. This was so cruel. So unfair.

"What is this?" she shouted, waving the drawing like a paper sword. "Some kind of bad joke?"

Her voice died in her throat when she realized the little girl had disappeared. There were no footprints in the snow. Debbie felt weak and supported herself on the railings. Tears rushed to her eyes. She looked at the drawing again, baffled—and then noticed the date on the lower left corner—it was today's date.

She wiped away tears with the back of her thumb and smiled at the empty street, the passing cars, and the weak sun trying to burn the corner of her eye as it rose over the roofs of the neighbors' houses.

Old Friends

ODIN'S HOUSE WAS a couple of miles west of Skagen, hidden by dunes of white sand and a forest of fir trees. It was a beautiful one-storey wooden structure, in typical '70s Danish style, with a large bay window and a flat roof.

Hermes parked the rental car in front, and the door of the house opened as he got out. The sky was a magnificent blue, with those golden reflections that made the region famous. It reminded Hermes of Greece, and he felt a pang of nostalgia grip his heart. He had been on the road for a long time now.

Freya stepped outside, as beautiful as he remembered her. She had taken the form of a middle-aged woman with large breasts and deep blue eyes that shone like sea-washed stones under her grayish blonde hair. She was casually dressed in jeans and a large men's shirt, but she was still as sexy as hell.

The Nordic Goddess of Love welcomed him with a long hug. Hermes enjoyed the large breasts pressing against his chest and the sweet perfume emanating from her body.

"A long time, Hermie."

Hermes nodded, taking a step back.

"Too long, Freya. Always too long."

"Come in. Odin's in his studio. He knew you would come."

Hermes smiled.

"Of course he did."

"Of course."

He followed her inside and they walked along the hallway until they reached a closed door. Freya was about to knock when they heard a loud "come in!" from the other side.

Odin stood in the middle of the room, in a stench of oil paint and turpentine. A canvas in progress was propped on an easel, others hung from the walls. Blank canvases of all sizes crowded the far side of the studio.

Hermes stepped carefully inside—he didn't want to ruin his nice Italian moccasins by trampling a paint tube. Freya sat on a wooden stool. Odin's good eye followed Hermes's movements carefully, while his glass eye remained still. The two gods embraced quietly.

"So, Hermie, this is it, then? Ragnarok?"

Looking around, Hermes shrugged. His sharp green eyes contrasted with Odin's piercing blue squint.

"I guess so. Not in the way we thought it would be though."

"Not in the way we feared it would be, you mean."

"I guess. But then again, we have no idea what's coming. It might be worse. That's why I'm visiting you. I like your paintings, by the way."

Odin turned to the unfinished piece on his easel.

"Thank you. I'm trying my best. The German tourists love them, but that's not surprising. I was their god once, after all."

They laughed.

Odin wiped his hands and Freya stood up.

"You want something to drink? A beer? Wine? Juice?"

"Thanks, a beer would be fine."

They sat around a paint spattered old table, while Freya took the chilled bottles from the studio fridge. Odin lit a small cigar.

"So, what's your feeling about all this?" he asked his Greek visitor.

Hermes sipped his beer.

"I don't know. I'm only a messenger. Right now, I'm gathering information."

"And . . . ?"

Odin's good eye was staring at him.

"And nobody really knows what to do. Whether we should move back or keep a low profile. Some want revenge, right here, right now. Some want to get back in business."

Odin blew out a small puff of blue smoke.

"It was a tough business. I think they've forgotten just how tough it was. You had to show your muscles all the time. Not good for the head. Made you crazy. Bad craziness."

The god of war hit his temple a couple of times to reinforce his words.

"I don't know if I want to go back in the business now. I like painting. And Freya likes living here. It's beautiful in the fall. Then again, if the space becomes available, why not? I know some of us might want to jump back in. I know Loki will. And Thor, of course. But as for me, I don't know. What does Zeus say?"

Hermes scratched at the wet label on his beer bottle with a careful finger.

"He's like you. Troubled. That's why he's sending me around. He thinks we should at least unite. Or work something out together. Forget the old rivalries."

Odin toyed with his thick beard and laughed out loud.

"Good old Zeus. Always the careful one. I'm sure Hera's behind this. Well, you can tell him he can call me whenever. Hell, he can even count on me, whatever happens. Not that it will make a difference now, will it? We're all in the same wagon, and it hasn't got any brakes. A curious situation, for us gods. Or retired gods. Whatever."

"Do you want to stay for diner?" Freya asked in her musical voice.

"No, thanks," Hermes replied politely. "I have a plane to catch at Billund tonight. In fact, I should be going now."

They walked to the car together. Odin gave Hermes a long hug and Freya kissed him on the corner of his lips, setting his nerves on fire.

"Let us know if anything happens," Odin said as Hermes sat behind the wheel. "You know where we live . . ."

"Sure. You'll be the first to know," he lied.

They waved until he disappeared at the first turn. Hermes felt a little melancholic. He thought Odin hadn't aged well. He'd looked much better with the old patch on his useless eye. The glass eye made him seem ridiculous.

Publish and Perish

"FUCK!"

GABE'S SWEARING woke Sid up.

Sid's mouth was caked with vomit and he stank like hell. He was about to tell Gabe to drive him home so he could take a goddamned shower when he realized that the building on fire beyond the police cars and firemen's trucks was his home. The flames roared high into the sky, illuminating the night and the surrounding buildings. Sid thought that—in a strange way—it was beautiful.

"I have to take you somewhere safe," Gabe said, revving the engine in reverse.

Sid was in a panic.

"Can you tell me what the hell is going on?" he squealed as the street spun round.

"The price of success," muttered Gabe between clenched teeth. "That's what's happening."

The car was racing through the maze of city streets at incredible speed and more than once Sid thought his last moment on earth had come.

"Where are we going?"

"Somewhere safe. At least I think it's safe."

What made Sid really nervous was the sweat that covered Gabe's face, shining under the city lights like a quicksilver mask. The editor was feeling sick again. Visions of Miss Jenkins's horrific death kept whirling in the back of his mind. Struck by lightning. In a garage. He couldn't believe it and yet it had happened. It had really happened. It all felt like a nightmare, but it was fucking real. And the smell . . . He clenched his teeth as he felt the bile surge back into his mouth.

"The only chance we have is that he thinks he's hit you," Gabe suddenly said, as he drove the car at full speed onto the expressway exchange. "He can't see that well anymore."

"He? Who's he?"

Gabe didn't answer but pointed at the sky. This was really getting out of hand. If he'd had the guts, Sid would have jumped from the car immediately. Unfortunately, he was half-covered in vomit and the car was doing about 110 mph.

"We have to make him believe you're dead, that he really killed you. It's the only way out. For you, at least."

"But . . . but . . . how?" Sid asked weakly.

"I've got an idea," Gabe said, taking the expressway to the northern part of the city. "Trust me."

Those were the last words of many a failed expedition, Sid thought, but he wisely kept it to himself. There was no need to anger the only psycho who could—maybe—help him stay alive. At least, for a while longer.

GOD SAYS:

DARK UNDER-EYE CIRCLES ARE INHERITED.

Black (Women) Power

AP — THE CITY of Lagos, Nigeria, is about to fall to the Pan-African Revolutionary Army of Women and hundreds of thousands of men have been seen fleeing the city. Since the beginning of the offensive last spring it is the third major city, after Onitsha and Benin City, to fall into the hands of the rebels, and it seems that the success of P.A.R.A.W is sending shockwaves throughout Africa. "There are reports of guerrilla warfare and local uprisings all across the continent," Pierre Cherruau, a French journalist specializing in African affairs, commented. "It seems that women in Nigeria have finally decided to do something for themselves and their country."

The declared aims of P.A.R.A.W are "to liberate women from the oppression of men, religion, and traditions, and to free the country from its state of economic slavery."

UN forces in Nigeria as peacekeepers have suffered heavy losses and it appears that support for P.A.R.A.W continues to grow at a phenomenal rate.

Foreign investors have warned that they will reconsider the future of their businesses in Nigeria if P.A.R.A.W gains control of the country.

"Let them leave," Aïssa Drame, the P.A.R.A.W spokesperson said. "We took care of our houses and our men for centuries without getting a single cent. Now we can take care of the entire land and finally get something out of it. It's only justice."

Publish or Perish

WHEN GABE OPENED the motel door Sid almost jumped through the ceiling. He'd spent the last two hours slouched on the bed, staring at the flickering TV screen, a dribble of spit hanging from his lower lip. Disconnected from the images, his brain ran its own strange program over and over again, like a bizarre screensaver. Memories from the last few months floated by and dissolved in a kaleidoscope of conflicting emotions and incredible pain. The million-dollar check. Houses in flames. Miss Jenkins's perfect body. Gabe walking into his office with the manuscript under his arm. The incredible sales. Tabago holding his chest as he collapsed on the ground. The flash of lightning and the disgusting ozone smell. And behind all that, a voice was shrieking: "What's going on? What's going on inside my head?" It was his own voice, incredibly high-pitched and ridiculous.

Gabriel stared at Sid and sighed. Sid lifted his hands as a sign of helplessness, not moving from the bed.

"I went to the mall and got some stuff," Gabe said in his usual professional tone. "If you want to have a chance to survive, put it on."

He threw the depressed publisher a plastic bag that landed on his stomach like a deflated football. Sid took it and warily peeked inside. Women's clothes and shoes. A blonde wig. Some makeup. This nightmare would never end.

"Jove's sight isn't what it used to be," Gabe explained, sitting on the bed and lighting a cigarette, "but he probably knows he missed you by now, and he's still looking . . . Better safe than sorry, right?"

Sid sat up, gathered the clothes, walked like a robot into the shiny bathroom, and began to undress. He felt like bursting into tears or laughing hysterically. Actually he did both. In the main room, he heard Gabe turn on his cell phone.

"It's me . . . I think we should talk this thing over . . . Yes, I know I'm not worried, it's just that . . . Yeah, you said that, that's true . . . Still, can you make it here? Things are getting a little more complicated than expected . . . We're at the Great Western, on 108, right off 96 . . . Yes. Fine, I'll wait."

Sid zipped up the back of his skirt. It was difficult and he had to use both hands. He looked at his fat hairy arms and wondered if he should shave them. Gabe hadn't said anything about that but it would improve the illusion, wouldn't it? Letting out a deep sigh, he ripped open the cellophane wrapper of the courtesy razor with his teeth.

Black Card

REUTERS — FOR THE first time in its history the World Cup soccer tournament has been cancelled due to disappointing ticket sales.

The Heavenly Corporation

STANDING IN FRONT of the large bay window of her new apartment overlooking the Petersburg skyline, Iris lights her joint and inhales deeply. She hasn't smoked grass in nearly a year now and she welcomes the familiar burn in her lungs. She's only wearing a light silk bathrobe over her naked body, and she feels a chill as she leans her shoulder against the window.

Visions of her past, the cleaning day job and the pitiful musical career, overlap in her reflection, diffused by the city's bright lights. What a long, strange trip it has been. Eddie's face appears, too, grinning. She'd met him by chance in the street yesterday, escorting another girl. She was black and had class—much more than Iris felt she'd ever had. Could be Eddie's lucky number. They'd exchanged a few words. He'd congratulated her on her new career. She'd thanked him for his time and patience. They'd separated and she'd not looked back. Not once. Now it made her feel funny. Not sad, not really. But strange. As if she'd seen a ghost.

She takes another hit, tries to relax.

Her reflection suddenly warps and the city disappears. It isn't night anymore and it is really hot. Oh, no, she thinks, here I go again. She'd hoped her visions were a thing of the past, but here she is now, in the middle of Africa or somewhere. She is surrounded by tall, dry yellow grass and can see a flat blue mountain in the distance. Some wind-twisted trees grow here and there, hosting cackling birds. She sees a strange pair of smallish apes, walking toward a large, sturdy tree. Heavy, round fruit hangs from its branches. Figs. Iris has always loved figs and those look delicious, ripe, and full of juice.

The apes stop at the foot of the tree and begin talking to each other. Of course, Iris can't understand a word of what they're saying, but she can understand that this is a language. The female has little tits pointing out through her brownish fur, while the male displays an impressive pair of furry balls. The female is obviously angry with the male for something, as she's shrieking at him and standing in his way.

The male extends a hand toward a fig, but the female slaps it away. She now seems to beg him, but the male is distracted, looking around, as if he's trying to spot someone or something. He finally pushes the female aside, throwing her to the ground, and jumps up to pluck the fruit.

As if on cue, a terrible lightning bolt strikes the tree, setting it on fire. The female jumps back, screaming while the male devours the fruit as if his life depends on it. More lightning strikes the ground a couple of feet away from the male. He begins to run away, followed by the female. Iris follows their progress for a while, as lightning bolts escort the fugitives.

As realization dawns as to what she has just seen, a single question enters her shocked mind: "Where was the snake?"

Old Friends

HERMES TOOK A look at his watch. He was wearing a white silk Paul Smith suit and sitting alone in front of a glass of wine in an expensive restaurant by the Sydney Opera House. Twelve forty-five. He wondered if Baiame had forgotten their appointment. It would be their first meeting and he was a little excited. Events were really shuffling the cards of Destiny. Everybody had been given a new deck, and they had to learn new rules. As the God of Crossroads, he felt perfectly at ease, although it was the first time he'd felt himself to be at the crossroads. Like when Pan had been declared dead, but for exactly the opposite reason. The paths had been narrowed then. Today, they were more numerous than ever before. Or so it seemed.

He took a sip of his 1960 Meursault and regretted that his sense of taste had disappeared. Two thousand years was a long time to heal. He was glad he was still alive. Some hadn't been so lucky. Baal, for example. Poor bastard. Jove had really done him in for good.

A handsome, dark-skinned man, dressed in a dark blue summer suit with a white shirt and black tie, entered the restaurant. He talked to the maître d' who politely pointed to Hermes. The man waved amiably and smiled as he came to the table. So this was Baiame, the Aboriginal Sky God, now working as the most popular weatherman for an Australian TV channel.

"Nice to meet you," Hermes said sincerely, shaking hands with his guest as he sat at the small, circular table.

"The same," Baiame said. "Sorry I'm a little late, but there were a few technical problems in the studio. Nothing I couldn't take care of myself, but I love to see the white man sweat a little, if you know what I mean."

They laughed. A waiter came and Baiame ordered a glass of 1967 Saint-Emilion.

"So, what brings you down under? I mean, I know Zeus sent you, but why?"

Hermes played with his glass, watching the golden liquid change hue as it moved in the light.

"My boss wants to know how the other partners are reacting to the hmm—changes."

Baiame grinned.

"Changes? What changes? For us nothing ever changes. We're still here. Working with our people. Interacting. Like the internet, but better. For real. Nothing virtual."

Hermes nodded. It was the first time he'd felt ill at ease with a colleague. Inadequate. He suddenly wondered why Zeus had sent him here. To be humiliated?

"I know your position is very different from ours. Zeus wants another perspective on things. To get a clearer view. So he can act better and not make a fool of himself. You know some are ready to come back with a vengeance. Not good. Others seem to have given up completely. Depressing. Zeus is very confused. I think he is afraid of imbalance. Uncontrolled situations. Things getting out of hand."

Baiame took a long sip from his glass.

"Control, lack of control. Who cares? Times are a-changing my friend. You have to go beyond that idea. Let things happen. Relax some. Man is going to discover a new world soon. His own world. Free. Go with the flow. Accept this freedom and there won't be any problem. No more control over things. A new time, made of past and present. Mixed. Transparent experiences. Like a river, except you can't see it. You can taste it, but you can't see it. Do you understand?"

Hermes nodded, although he wondered how he was going to explain this to the boss. Zeus had always been a little obtuse. Philosophy had never been one of his strengths.

He lifted his glass as Baiame was checking the menu brought by a beautiful waitress. She had red, waist-length hair, gathered in an incredibly lush ponytail, and her breasts, compressed in her uniform, looked very promising. The wine flowed over Hermes's tongue and suddenly he had the impression that he could taste it. It was weak, like an ember in the wind, but it was definitely there. Sweet, round, golden. Taste! Hermes stared at Baiame who was pointing at the menu asking what various dishes were. An aroma drifted to his nostrils, a mingling of sweat and perfume. The waitress. She saw him staring at her and smiled. He smiled back, transfixed. Something warm filled the front of his pants. This trip had been worth it after all.

Publish and Perish

THERE WAS A loud rap on the door and Gabe stood up and went to open it. Lying on the bed, sweating under his wig, Sid picked up the remote control and muted the TV.

Gabe let a small scrubby figure scuttle in, long gray hair hanging in front of his face. The man was wearing a dirty, cut-up jean jacket, showing sinewy arms and ring-covered hands. His jeans were soiled with motor oil and Sid saw the thick black handle of a gun sticking out from behind a tarnished silver belt buckle.

"Shut the fucking door," the man mumbled to Gabe as he looked around the room. He stared at Sid, his coal black eyes locked on him in a scrutinizing gaze.

"Who's the broad?" he asked Gabe, not taking his eyes off Sid.

A shiver of fear ran down Sid's spine. The man's sharp-featured face was dark, and the goatee didn't make him look any less threatening. Sid thought of a mad biker.

"It's Saperstein, the publisher, my Lord."

My Lord? Sid thought. This is getting weirder and weirder.

"Why is he dressed like a girl?"

Gabe crossed his arms over his chest.

"That's part of the problem, my Lord. Jove almost got him and I thought it best to try and keep him out of harm's way."

The Lord thoughtfully scratched his beard. Sid suddenly noticed the enormous round scars on his wrists. Ugly things.

"Hmmm, maybe. What's going on, anyway? How are we doing?"

Gabe grinned.

"Fine, just fine. Apart from the schedule problem. Other than that, the operation is a complete success. Millions of books sold. Debates all over. I think you can come out soon and reveal yourself to the world. It's about ready."

"Got anything to drink? I think we should celebrate."

Gabe walked over to the mini-fridge.

"Gin and tonic, as usual?"

The Lord nodded distractedly. He was still looking at Sid, who sat motionless, the remote still in his hand.

"Can't wait to make that fucker pay," the man said. "He owes me. Big. Must be feeling the pressure now, the bastard."

Gabe nodded as he fixed the drink.

"Yes, my Lord. But he's reacting fast. Almost killed our friend here."

"Jove has always been trigger-happy. That's exactly what I've been counting on since we started the operation. Make him nervous so he sticks his big head out and then—Bang! Bang! Bang!"

Gabe handed him the plastic glass. Sid thought he could use a drink too, but didn't dare ask. The man gave a chilling laugh, raised the glass to his lips.

"Think about that, Gabe. I'm the Anti-Christ. Me. Yeshuah. Fucking St. John didn't think about that one, uh? Major fuck-up in the prophecy, Mr. Jove. Dad. Fucker."

He gulped the drink down and wiped his chin. His piercing gaze landed back on Sid.

"Put his normal clothes back on, Gabe."

Gabe looked confused.

"But why, my Lord?"

Yeshuah's face twisted into an angry grimace.

"Because he's our fucking bait, that's why. We need Jove to find him, so we can waste the bastard. So give him his fucking clothes back and drive him somewhere Jove can find him. Like a church. Or a synagogue. Or a mosque, for all I care. Somewhere obvious. Get it?"

Gabe nodded and opened the closet.

Sid hung his head. There was no end to this nightmare. Next time he signed a contract, it would be with the Devil. At least you knew what to expect.

GOD SAYS:

THE AUTHOR WHO MADE VERMEER A
POP PHENOM IMAGINES THE EARTHLY
INSPIRATIONS THAT FUELLED WILLIAM
BLAKE'S VISIONARY EXALTATIONS

Old Friends

HERMES FELT A little drunk, his ears filled with the round melodies of the electronic bossa nova filling up the nightclub. Standing at the bar, he watched the packed crowd dancing sensuously to the artificial beat, bathed in the pink and blue lights that whirled above the dance floor. He loved this club. It was Brasilia's most exclusive place, occupying the entire roof terrace of an Oscar Niemeyer building located only a few streets away from the famous Palace of the People.

Although his senses weren't what they had once been, progress had been incredible. He could taste almost everything now and his nose captured random fragrances. They were still difficult to identify, but day after day, names and origins returned to his mental catalogue. As for touch . . . He closed his eyes, humming to the music. Flashes of his recent stay in Sydney appeared behind his closed eyelids in Technicolor*.

Soft white breasts. Pale pink nipples hardening under his hands. Sensuous hips turning into magical thighs.

Her stomach, lifting rhythmically under his thrusts. Her moisture under his tongue. The shooting star of pleasure firing up from his loins. Cosmic peace. The pleasure of a cigarette. Again.

He would never forget the Australian waitress. She was his gateway into a world renewed. He wondered if she was pregnant with the first demigod of the next generation. The thought made him smile as he reached for his cigarettes.

A hand suddenly grabbed his shoulder. He recognized the grip and turned smiling. Dressed in a revealing black polo shirt over black Armani pants and matching crocodile shoes, Jerry looked absolutely divine.

"What took you so long?" the Greek god asked the newcomer.

"Time, what else?"

Jerry Cornelius, the famous assassin-diplomat, time-traveler extraordinaire, and a familiar presence since the dawn of western civilization, smiled in his turn and ordered a Sapphire and tonic. Although quite tipsy now, Hermes knew he shouldn't let his guard down. With Jerry, you never knew what to expect. He was known to be able to travel forward in time, although it was physically impossible. Even gods couldn't enter the Gates of the Future, although they were ahead of men by a few seconds, a minute, a day. But just that, nothing more. Even Pythia couldn't see beyond that. Of course, a few seconds could change everything. That's why you had to be careful with Jerry.

"Who are you working for these days?" Hermes asked, turning his gaze back to the dancers. He was hesitating between a young, mannish boy with black curls dripping with sweat and a blonde Scandinavian-type beauty in a miniskirt, dancing barefoot.

Jerry shrugged the question off, taking a delicate sip of his drink.

"Times are changing. I'm taking the temperature."

"Are you worried?"

Jerry turned his beautiful gaze upon Hermes who shivered inside. They had already slept together once and he would do it again, if it wasn't so dangerous. Zeus would kill him if anything changed in his plans.

"I'm never worried. Curious, yes. Always have been, always will be."

Hermes decided it would be safer to play an open hand.

"What do you want to know? You're here for a reason."

Jerry raised a perfect eyebrow and shrugged.

"Moi?"

He laughed. It sounded like champagne filling up a chilled glass.

"Okay, I'll be honest with you. You know me."

He winked. Hermes nodded, feeling his charm.

"Are the signs for real?"

The question surprised the god.

"Who wants to know?"

"Me. Who else?"

Hermes tried to interpret Jerry's look, but it was pure, bottomless black.

"Pythia thinks they are."

Jerry pondered the answer.

"But she's not certain?"

"Who can be?"

Hermes was happy he could beat Jerry at his own game. It didn't happen often. Loki had managed it once and still talked about it with pride. Jerry hummed a few bars, nodding.

"That's all you're going to tell me?"

"Yes. It's more than enough already."

Jerry put his drink on the bar and leaned closer. Hermes closed his eyes. Jerry's wonderful lips closed over his, and Hermes felt the tip of Jerry's tongue trying to pass through his own clenched teeth.

"Some other time, maybe?" The assassin asked, stroking Hermes's cheek.

"With pleasure."

Hermes watched his friend disappear through the dancing crowd. He felt a pang of regret and a twinkle of pride. Yes, times were definitely changing. He had resisted Jerry. He was back in business.

The Heavenly Corporation

ALTHOUGH HER BODY felt completely relaxed Iris couldn't fall asleep. In the darkness of the room she could still distinguish the familiar shapes of her furniture and artwork hanging on the walls. The city lights glimmered through the fabric of the thin curtains, moving with the evening breeze. She needed a cigarette, but her pack was in the sitting room and right now that felt like miles away. She could hear the faint whispering of the traffic outside, accompanying her thoughts.

She had never felt so good in her life, and it wasn't because of her success, although she had just signed a nationwide contract with PCTV for a weekly morning show. Yes, things had rocketed upward since her cleaning-woman debut in Petersburg and her failed attempts at singing. She smirked in the darkness. The only thing she hoped was that nobody would find an old tape of Show Me Yours and I'll Show You Mine and put in on the Net. That would be so embarrassing. The show was still on, but she hadn't watched it since her own humiliating session. No need to scratch an old wound.

The nicotine craving became unbearable and she had to get out of bed. She felt a chill as she trotted to the sitting room and hurried back to the warm bedroom with her treasure in hand. The quick flame almost blinded her as she lit the cigarette and let the gray smoke pour out of her nose like a transparent waterfall. Her body felt heavier and heavier and she reclined against the wall. It should have been illegal to feel so good.

Frankie was sleeping next to her, arms stretched upward, beautiful breasts slightly sagging on both sides. Iris felt like biting them again, then sucking and licking, as she had done the whole evening after coming back from the restaurant. And Frankie's mouth, half open now and slightly snoring . . . When Frankie had kissed her in the elevator it was as if Iris's whole life had suddenly made sense, as if a stranger's hand had managed to click all the pieces of her puzzle together—and it felt great. Wonderful. Exciting.

She had never imagined that she would fall in love with a woman, but then Frankie was also a great person. She smelled good and she was a sensual kisser, lover, soul mate.

Frankie laughed in her sleep. Iris grinned, then took a long drag on her cigarette, making the tip glow harder in the darkness. Maybe she couldn't see the future, but she could certainly enjoy the present. Second after second, minute after minute. And, for once, it felt wonderful not to know what was going to happen next.

Dust to Dust

AP — CONCERN IS growing around the world as paper money, coins, and even silver and gold are attacked by a previously unknown parasite that causes them to crumble and flake into worthless fragments.

First reported in Eastern Europe and explained as an elaborate hoax, the parasite spread quickly to Russia, China, and Western Europe.

Monetary losses are expected to run into billions of dollars, but as the crisis is still evolving, no national government has yet been able to publish confirmed figures.

Banks have been besieged by hysterical crowds and an unprecedented wave of related suicides has been reported.

The parasite now appears to have reached America, where major cities including New York, Washington, and Philadelphia have reported outbreaks of the contamination. The National Guard has been put on alert across the country, in order to help deal with the kind of panic and mass hysteria recently reported by European broadcasters.

The President will address the nation at 7 p.m. tonight from his bunker beneath the White House.

Publish and Perish

SID WAS FURIOUS as he pulled on his pants under the scrutiny of Yeshuah and Gabe. He had shaved his entire body for nothing, and he felt like a goddamned fool. He hadn't yet removed his dress and his wig was falling across his eyes, half-blinding him. The only positive aspect of this ridiculous situation was that he did not have to wear those white high-heeled shoes and would be able to put his normal shoes back on.

Right then the door burst open with a deafening crash and the splintering of wood. S.W.A.T! Sid thought as he jumped like a startled rabbit behind the king-size bed, landing heavily on the thinly carpeted floor.

"You!"

He heard Yeshuah's voice, filled with surprise and anger. Sid carefully raised his head, tugging his wig into place so he could see what was going on. An old man in a wheelchair had entered the room, pushed by someone who appeared to be Gabe's twin brother, a large, tall, Nazi look-alike. The old man, dressed in an immaculate white suit, wore his silvery hair shoulder-length and had a goatee and a pair of '50s Ray-Ban sunglasses. Colonel Sanders, Sid thought.

"Yes. Aren't you glad we finally meet again?"

The voice was melodious and strong.

"You!" Yeshuah repeated, apparently shocked.

As quick as a flash he freed the gun from his pants and pointed it at the invalid, who laughed.

"Did you see that, Michael? That's my son, all right. Always so prompt to react. That's what I've always liked about him. We could have done so many beautiful things together . . ."

"And you fucked it all up, you crazy bastard!" Yeshuah yelled.

"You heard that? You heard that?" The old man began to laugh again. "I . . . I fucked it up? That's too funny! I fucked it up!"

Slapping his thighs as if possessed by his own mirth, the old man reached down and Sid saw him pull out a gun similar to Yeshuah's from inside his boot. As if on cue, Gabe and his clone also drew their pieces. Tarantino, Sid thought, torn between his curiosity and the fear of a stray bullet.

Yeshuah's face showed tremendous pain.

"Why? Why have you forsaken me?" His hand was trembling, but he didn't lower his gun.

The old man shrugged.

"You know why. You never listened to me. Not once."

"You didn't have to kill me. You didn't kill Muhammad."

The old man sighed. Gabe and his clone remained perfectly still, like two statues.

"Muhammad was a good boy. He obeyed. He did everything I told him to. You, on the other hand . . ."

A grimace of spite distorted the lower part of his face. Yeshuah let out a defiant high-pitched laugh.

"Why would I obey you? Where were you all the time, when I was doing your business? Up there, living the good life. You didn't come down once. You didn't talk to me once and you wonder why I took my chance? I mean, all those people, waiting for something and I was supposed to give them to you? And what about me, dad? What about me?"

"Whoa! Wait a minute! What about all those miracles I sent you, you fucking ungrateful son of a bitch?"

"Those miracles were mine, dad! I made them! You were too busy doing your thing up there—you never helped me once! You're just a selfish, narcissistic, power-crazed, senile old man!"

Sid could see that the cheeks of the old man had turned a fiery red as he cocked his gun.

"I killed you once. I can kill you again."

Yeshuah grinned and cocked his gun in turn.

"I can kill you too. Took me two thousand years to heal and make a comeback. I'm curious to see how long it'll take you."

The old man smiled coyly.

"Well, why don't we find ou—"

The simultaneous firing of four guns was deafening and Sid dropped to the ground like a trembling sack of grain. "Oh my God! Oh my God!" he repeated over and over, half-conscious of the absurdity of his own words. Face down, hands over his head, he waited for further developments, but to his surprise nothing happened. Cautiously raising his head above the bed, he instantly froze at the sight of the four bodies sprayed with red and scattered in various positions around the room.

Nervously, Sid stood up. He was barefooted and he gagged when he felt the blood's warm moisture under his toes. Yeshuah was slouched against Gabe's body. The bullets had torn a big hole in his chest. Half of Gabe's skull was missing. Sid turned to the old man, who had a huge black hole under the left eye. Michael was on his back, his white suit repainted red by an amateur hand. None of the four appeared to be breathing. Time and space stood still. Sid removed his wig, fell on his knees, and began to sob hysterically. He was still crying when the cops appeared at the door.

An Olympic Tragedy
Part Two

"WELL, FRANK, SEEMS we finally have the translation of Hou Tsi's words . . ."

"That's interesting, Steve. What did he say? I'm sure all our viewers are very curious to hear that."

"Well, Frank, it doesn't really make sense . . . I mean . . . hell, here we go anyway, he said: 'The great god Pan is back.'"

"The what?"

"The great god Pan. Never heard of him. Must be a Chinese deity of some sort."

"Not the deity of diving, in any case."

"Ha, ha, ha! No, you're right about that one, Frank! Okay, who do we have next . . . ?"

"Norbert Legrand, a Frenchman."

"Let's see if their diving is as good as their cooking . . ."

Bad News

THE HOLY MAN had his back turned to him, looking through the window onto the beautiful park outside. He was dressed in white and the evening sun created a golden halo around him.

Jerry Cornelius cleared his throat once to announce his presence and noticed a familiar paperback on the Pope's table. The Italian version of the infamous Gospel According to Jesus. He wondered what the holy man thought of it. Then again, he already knew. The robed figure didn't budge as Jerry took a step closer, but a tilting of his head indicated that he was aware of his presence.

"So, my dear friend, what news do you bring?"

The voice was soft and empowering. Perfect for the job, Jerry thought as he moved closer, only separated from his host by a couple of feet now.

"Not very good, I'm afraid. For you, anyway. Everything has been confirmed. My sources are adamant."

The holy man turned around, frowning.

"Everything?"

"Yes, your holiness. Sorry I couldn't do anything about it, but we were warned too late. We should have paid more attention to that book . . ."

Jerry's eyes glanced at the pocketbook on the table, the Pope turned toward him, his eyes still, dark and thoughtful.

"Is there, hmm . . . someone else behind all this?"

Jerry took the hint and shook his head.

"I'm afraid not, your holiness. Pure chaos this time. The best kind, if you pardon my French. Unpredictable series of events, themselves predicted, but wrongly, as in most cases. A lesson to all."

The old man took a step closer and grabbed Jerry Cornelius's arm, a whiff of cologne suddenly reached the assassin-diplomat's nostrils. Acqua di Parma, of course.

"Can't you do anything? I mean, maybe it's not too late. You could travel back in time, perhaps, I don't know, about a day or two only and change things. Kill someone, put things back on their normal track . . ."

Jerry stepped back, liberating himself from the iron grip, desperately shaking his arm.

"My services end here, your holiness. I tried my best to help you, but you know I myself am a child of chaos. So when chaos triumphs, I must abide . . . Farewell then, and good luck."

Jerry was about to turn around when the old man seized his arm again, his mouth opening and closing like a fish, obviously at a loss for words.

"But . . . what am I supposed to do?"

Jerry Cornelius thought about the thousands of doors opening at the same time, at this very second. Even more would open in a couple of minutes, and so on. An infinite number. Back to possibilities, and the end of probabilities. A breath of fresh air, although working for the Pope had been fun. He'd always enjoyed working on hopeless situations.

"Jerry," the man gasped again. "What am I going to do?"

The diplomat-assassin looked at him, his face suddenly distant and blank.

"Like they say in my favorite James Bond movie: 'Improvise, my dear friend, im-pro-vise.'"

He tapped the old man on the shoulder, then turned around and left the room. In the long white marble corridor, he began to whistle a beautiful melody he thought he had forgotten eons ago.

The Walls of Jerusalem

AP — A DEVASTATING earthquake shook Jerusalem this morning, destroying the Al-Aqsa mosque, the Wailing Wall, and other holy sites, as well as leaving thousands dead and an unknown number homeless.

Scientists still cannot explain the origin of the earthquake, measuring 9 on the Richter scale, as Israel is not situated on any of the region's major fault lines.

Publish and Perish

COMFORTABLY SEATED AT an outside table of the Café Kropotkin, Sid put down the newspaper he was reading and took a long sip of his steaming black coffee, feeling relaxed for the first time in ages.

He'd spent the last twenty-four hours at Petersburg's central police station, telling the force a ridiculous story about having been kidnapped by crazy cult members who had finally shot each other in a bad case of drug-induced paranoia. The pigs had bought the story, as had the press.

The headline of that morning's Petersburg Herald read: PUBLISHING MOGUL HELD HOSTAGE BY DRUG-CRAZED CULT MEMBERS. He smiled to himself. All was well that ended well. Except for Miss Jenkins, of course, God bless her soul. She would be hard to replace . . . So many good memories . . . And a mouth . . . But he was a rich man now, with endless possibilities open to him.

He glanced at the thick line of panicked customers waiting their turn to enter the Petersburg National Bank office at the corner of the street. Some first-class hoax about money disappearing was running around. Genius. An Orson Welles of his own kind, only a little more dramatic. Although the media had explained that it was, indeed, a very well-thought-out hoax, people still panicked, sending stock markets up and down on a hellish rollercoaster. This morning, on the radio, he'd heard that the police had shot 27 people in São Paulo in front of the First National Bank. Incredible what people wanted to believe. Hell, he sure knew about that now. Still, he would call his own bank in the Bahamas later in the afternoon, just to make sure. He just loved those guys' accents and over-politeness. He could hear them — "No problem, sir, thank you, sir, at your service, sir . . ."

A bright, cloudless future was ahead of him, singing his name. He was only missing the choir of Angels, but then again, as Gabe had taught him, couldn't money buy anything?

GOD SAYS:

LIFE. LIBERTY. AND THE PURSUIT.

The Heavenly Corporation

IRIS WAS LED into a small room crammed with works of art. She had never been in a Renaissance palace before and was completely astounded by the beauty and refinement displayed all around her.

The chamber held a small table and two cushioned oak chairs. She placed her handbag on the table, not knowing whether she should stand or sit. She finally decided to look at the collection of small, framed paintings that adorned the room's wood-paneled walls. The names inscribed on the copper tags reminded her of school visits to the Babylon museum of art. Tintoretto, Raffaello, Veronese . . .

A muffled sound made her look round. An old man dressed in white with a golden silk cummerbund around his waist stood alone at the door. He looked kind but ill at ease, which she could perfectly understand.

"I am grateful you could come," he said, his voice soft and low, with a slight Italian accent. "I have heard a lot about you."

"I have heard a lot about you too," Iris joked, immediately regretting it.

Blushing, she curtsied, not knowing if it was the right thing to do. All had happened so suddenly. The telephone call. The man at the door. Dark glasses mandatory, they'd insisted. The private jet. The hotel room. The night ride through Rome in a limousine. Now here at last. Wow! What a trip.

The holy man extended his hands, in a welcoming gesture. Iris reached for his fingers and closed her eyes.

She saw his holiness carefully coming out of the shower, a white towel around his waist. He suddenly slipped, lost his balance, and fell backward onto the shower taps. He winced and as he stood back up Iris could see that his back was badly bruised.

She whispered what she had just seen into his holy ear and he stared at her with a mixture of embarrassment and respect.

"That confirms what I have heard about you," he said, showing her to the table. "Let's begin the session . . ."

Nodding, Iris took the cards out of her bag.

La Liberté

THE MAN SEEMED to have appeared from nowhere. Dressed in an old-fashioned general's uniform, his gold medals and braid shone hard under the merciless Haitian noon sky. He even had a matching hat, adorned with white feathers and a long sword hanging from his side. American soldiers were strolling casually on the nearby quay. The corporal who noticed him first nudged his sergeant.

"Look at the loony," he said.

They all laughed, shook their heads in disbelief, and carried on with their patrol. This country was just too much. Crazies everywhere.

The "general" called to a docker smoking a cigarette, who approached him carefully. They exchanged a few words in Creole and the man gave him directions. The "general" thanked him and the man shuffled away as if he was on a mission.

The corporal turned around once more, glancing at the colorful silhouette walking toward the city limits.

A few passersby had joined him, chanting and clapping their hands. The soldier first thought they were mocking the strange character, but he seemed happy and enthusiastic.

"Harding! What the fuck you doing?"

The corporal turned his head and saw the patrol had stopped about a hundred feet away, waiting for him. He raised his arm to show them he'd heard, but didn't bring it down. The crowd had grown thicker—you could only see the loony's feathers sticking up—and they were singing and clapping their hands louder and louder.

"Toussaint est revenu! Toussaint est revenu!"

"What the hell are they singing, Harding?"

The sergeant's voice startled him.

"Should we call for reinforcement?"

Harding looked at the colorful human snake growing by the minute and moving downtown at incredible speed.

"Toussaint est revenu! Toussaint est revenu!"

"Hell, I don't know, Sarge. Can't figure out what they're singing. It wasn't anything they taught me on the crash course."

The soldiers stood there for a while under the crushing sun, until their eyes were blurred by the sweat dripping from beneath their heavy helmets and they resumed their patrol, shaking their heads, laughing at this crazy island filled with crazy people.

Old Friends

DRESSED IN A white Yves Saint-Laurent linen suit with matching Panama hat, Hermes came into Omonia Square and looked around, feeling incredibly happy. He had always loved Athens in the summer. Crushed under the blazing eye of Apollo, the city seemed to fight back with noise, bad smells, and a generally bad attitude.

Reaching for his cigarettes in the inside pocket of his jacket, he pulled out a pack of Player's Navy Cut. The bitter taste of the tobacco deliciously tickled his tongue and throat. It was wonderful to be back in business. A group of teenage girls flocked around him, eyeing him curiously. He smiled at them, but they didn't smile back. Oh, well, things would take their normal course again, eventually. No need to hurry. No need to worry. Feel free. Be free. That's what he'd told Zeus earlier that morning as he'd handed him his resignation. The face of the passé god! Could do his PR work himself now, the old fart. Yes, times were definitely a-changing.

Still waiting for the lights to change, Hermes took a deep breath just as a gust of wind lifted up and swept through the streets, making everyone dizzy with the mixed scents of jasmine and roses.

SEB DOUBINSKY is a French bilingual writer, born in 1963 in Paris. He has published more than 15 novels and 6 poetry collections in France, the UK, and the USA. His fiction can be seen as a mosaic of different styles and subjects, although it is always centered on questions of freedom and identity. He currently lives and teaches in Aarhus, Denmark, with his wife and their two children.